The Trouble With Fiction

AZARIA RENTOUL

PUBLISHER
Azaria Rentoul
Prebbleton, New Zealand

ISBN: 978-0-473-71953-1 (Softcover)

Any references to historical events, real people, or real places are used fictitiously. Names, characters, and places are products of the author's imagination.

Front cover image by Lia Kammerer
Book design by Azaria Rentoul

First edition 2024

Publisher: Azaria Rentoul
5 Pointsman Place
Prebbleton, New Zealand
7604

Dedicated to my awesome friends who literally wouldn't let me give up.

Table of Contents

WRITER'S NOTE AND ACKNOWLEDGMENTS

Writing a book is *waaaaay* harder than I used to think. It used to be 'Oh, I'll just stick a bunch of words into coherent sentences for about ten pages in a row and call it a book.' Now I realize that that's not even close to a book. A story, yes, but a book? Definitely not.

This book was formulated over many months and took a lot of trial and error and careful planning. Honestly, there were times when I thought I would never finish. And once I did finish, I thought this book was terrible. But my mother managed to convince me otherwise and here it is. A proper book.

Here's hoping I can write another one.

And now for that part in every book that most people don't even bother to read but authors are obliged to write anyway. The acknowledgments.

First, I would like to thank my mother, for editing the very raw copy of the book. I'd also like to thank my little brother and my oma for helping with the editing process as well. I'd like to thank my older brother and my dad for coming up with some very creative suggestions for the story and the title.

Thank you to Makayla and Megan for being very encouraging and not letting me give up on this book. It probably wouldn't have been finished without you.

And a huge thank you to Lia for creating the absolutely incredible front cover image. Literally amazing.

PROLOGUE

Weak winter sunlight shone in through the windows of a quiet bookshop. The shop was empty, apart from the shelves of books and a tired looking man behind the counter. Sighing slightly as he gazed around the aisles, the man picked up the book that he was reading, *The Hunger Games*, and opened it. He had only just read a few pages, when there was a cheerful tinkle from the bell above the door. The man glanced up as a woman entered his shop. Removing her gloves, the woman gave the man behind the counter a friendly smile and strode over to browse the books. As she did, she knocked a rather thick book with a green and gray cover off the discount shelf. Bending down, she grasped the book and glanced at the cover. It depicted a glaring woman, drawn in gray and green, with long wild hair and a faded green robe. The woman held a staff with a misty gray globe on the end. The title was *The Adventure Story of Ellie and Glorathy Dodge*.

Flicking through it, the woman wrinkled her nose, and replaced the book on the shelf. She continued down the aisle.

CHAPTER ONE
Cassie Undering

Brrrrrring! The bell rang, loud and clear in my ears, snapping me out of my daydream.

"I hope you all have a great weekend, class!" said Mr Brown, the most enthusiastic teacher at our school, clapping and giving a cringe-worthy grin.

Emily Jonas, one of the bright-eyed students who gets the best grades and wears the largest glasses I have ever seen, cheered. When no one else joined in, she flushed pink and looked down at her desk. Jared Bailey, the boy who sits behind me, whispered something to Dylan Green. It was probably a nasty comment about Emily's 'Bee Happy' t-shirt. Both boys laughed quietly.

"Remember to team up for your group assignment. Monday we have a math quiz, so study hard!" Mr Brown continued, his wide grin not failing, "Dismissed!"

The classroom filled with the hoots and hollers of excited rugby boys, who were ready to head to practice. I waited while they raced out first. Carefully, I tidied my things as the rest of my class slowly headed out after the boys. The last few to leave were Katelyn Johnson and Josie Peters. Katelyn glanced at me as she headed out. She stalled for a split second, as if she were going to ask me to join them. But Josie said something to her and both girls laughed. Then they were gone. I breathed an inaudible sigh of relief. At least I did not have to think of some excuse to refuse Katelyn's offer. I hated it when people thought it was sad that I was alone. I worked by myself and I liked it that way.

"Ah, Cassie," Mr Brown said, looking up and smiling at me. "Always last, eh? I have been meaning to talk to you about your participation in group projects."

I frowned. Sure, I did not like working with a group and often asked for an exception. So what? I preferred working alone. Less complicated.

"I feel that you just won't connect with other students if you insist on working alone," Mr Brown continued.

The last thing I wanted was my teacher worrying about my social life. My sister did that enough. "I'm fine," I said.

Mr Brown gave another encouraging smile. "What about if I pair you up with Katelyn? You used to beg to be put in the same group."

I shook my head, maybe a little too violently. The key words in that sentence were 'used to' and I wasn't going to let Mr Brown skip over that. "I like working alone," I told him.

Mr Brown gave a sigh, the closest he got to sounding disappointed. "Alright, Cassie, if you insist. Off you go."

I nodded and hurried off. Racing down the nearly empty hallways to my locker, I spotted another girl heading the opposite way. She was clearly new, obvious by the spotless uniform and bent head. As I approached, she looked up. Locking eyes with me, she gave a hesitant smile. I almost smiled back, but she might think I wanted to talk to her. Instead, I broke eye contact and hurried on. Trust me, the last thing I needed was friends.

I always walked from school straight to archery, which was at a farm near the edge of town, close to the hills. It was a twenty minute walk from school. My instructor, Kelly, was waiting at the gates when I arrived. A small bus was just pulling up, kids from the local primary school inside.

"Jamie's taking the after-school kids to the field range today," Kelly informed me. "You and I are in the woods." I nodded. Jamie Gadaway, Kelly's dad, had been running archery classes at his farm for as long as I could remember. Kelly, who was nineteen, always helped out when she didn't have lectures. Hamish, Kelly's brother, who went to my school, sometimes joined in as well.

Kelly led me over to the shed where the bows were stored and grabbed her one from its place on the wall. I selected the one I usually used and followed her across the paddocks to the little section of forest that is part of the farm. The set up was familiar. A series of stiff foam targets, some large, like the deer and the bear, and some smaller, like the rabbits and possums. The place you stood on to shoot was a raised wooden platform with loose rope fences surrounding it. Attached to the three front posts were quivers full of arrows.

"You got the bullseye last time," Kelly said, gesturing to the generic old target also set up near the back of the range. "What's the goal now?"

"Consistently get the bullseye," I muttered.

"And how are you going to do that?" Kelly asked, one eyebrow raised.

"Practice," I said, stepping up to the mark and choosing one of the long, straight arrows. I was deliberately short. I hated it when Kelly tried to make conversation with me. It would be better if she didn't. I wouldn't have to keep fending her off. I was sure I sounded like a grumpy self absorbed teenager, but I didn't want the hassle of friends. Not even nice older ones, who liked archery as much as me.

I zoned out my surrounding, bringing my bow up into position and stretching the arrow back so it was in line with my ear. Not too far. Kelly disappeared. So did the trees and the platform. Just me and the target. I fired.

Twang!

My arrow lodged deep into the middle ring of the target with a dull thud, one out from the bullseye. Kelly gave it a 'meh' sort of stare. "Not bad. You can do better."

I picked another arrow and drew it back. As I was readying myself to shoot, I saw something strange out of the corner of my eye. A very faint fizzing noise filled my ears as a small swirling purple cloud seemed to appear out of thin air. It grew wider and wider until some sort of gap opened in the middle of the purple cloud and I could see what appeared to be blue sky. The cloud hovered there for a moment before something fell out of it and thudded gently onto the leaf litter of the forest floor. The cloud vanished with a barely audible pop. It surprised me so much that I let go. My arrow went flying towards the target and hit the tree behind it.

Kelly, who didn't appear to have seen the mysterious purple cloud, frowned. "Way off. Try again, Cassie." Instead of choosing a new arrow, I stepped off the platform and bent down to pick up the object that had fallen out of the cloud. It was a shoe. A very fancy shoe with a high heel and a dainty shape to it. Even more surprisingly it was made entirely of glass!

"What's that?" Kelly asked, looking over my shoulder.

I turned and showed her. "A glass shoe."

Kelly frowned. "Was that here when we got here?"

I shrugged. For some reason, the fact that Kelly hadn't seen the purple cloud or heard the pop, made me not want to mention it. Had I just imagined it? What if Kelly thought I was making it up? What if she thought I was crazy?

"Maybe one of the kids yesterday thought it would be funny to leave it here as a joke," Kelly said, her brow furrowing further. "I'll tell Dad to keep a better eye on them."

I tried to hand her the glass shoe, but she waved it away. "You keep it. I don't need it." I didn't bother pointing out that I didn't need it either, I just stuffed it into my school bag.

"So, how did it go today?" my older sister, Chloe, asked when I plopped into the passenger seat of her car. She revved the engine and pulled out into the road.

"School was okay," I said truthfully. "Archery was fun."

"Make any new friends?" Chloe asked, sounding hopeful. She always asked that.

I shook my head. "I don't need any friends, Chloe. I have you and Dad and Copper. That's enough." Chloe's cheerful smile faded a little and for a moment I felt a pang of guilt. Then it was gone.

"What about Katelyn?" Chloe tried. "You used to be great friends before… it happened."

"You can say it you know Chloe," I snapped. "It's not like I don't know that Mum's dead." Chloe flinched a little and I instantly felt bad.

"Sorry," I muttered.

"Ever since Mum died, you've been alone most of the time, Cass," Chloe said. "It's been two years. I feel like you should move on." I turned away from my sister, but she kept talking. "You do need to move on Cassie. Mum's gone and there's nothing we can do about it. We all miss her but we just have to keep going. Make new friends and try new things. It isn't that hard." I squeezed my eyes shut as the involuntary tears threatened to show. An unwelcome memory barged its way into my mind.

I stood at my mother's bedside, watching her laboured breathing. Chloe, her blue eyes wide and sad, grabbed my hand and squeezed. My other hand held onto my mother's weak and pale one. "I'm sorry," the doctor told my dad. "There's nothing more we can do. We've tried everything."

Dad squeezed his eyes shut for a moment, then opened them again, glancing over at us. "Alright."

"You have a few hours maybe, to say goodbye," the doctor murmured, scurrying out of the room.

"Mum?" I said in a tiny voice, my grip on my mother's hand tightening. Her eyes, once such a sparkling blue, were now dull. It was like the cancer had sucked the colour out of her. She tried to lift her head, but was too weak. Her smile seemed too sad.

"My girls," she said, her voice just a whisper.

My tears threatened to fall as I met her gaze. I could no longer see the cheerful, joyful person she used to be, with long golden brown hair and laughter in her blue gaze. Instead, that was all overshadowed by the pale, bald Mum who lay in the bed, too weak to do anything but try and keep going.

Dad moved around the bed to stand beside Chloe and Mum gave him a smile. "It's time," she breathed. "I can feel it."

"No," I choked out. "You can't go! Please!" My last word came out in a whimper.

"Cassie," Mum whispered, "My little baby girl. I'm so sorry." Her gaze drifted to Chloe and Dad. "I love you all so much -" She broke off as her breath caught.

"Mum," Chloe told her, "you don't have to talk. Just rest." Mum closed her eyes and drifted off. I don't know how long we sat there, listening to the muffled sounds of work going on and watching Mum sleep. It felt like an eternity. Every time Mum's breathing paused I thought it was over. We all stayed; me, Dad, and Chloe. I had wanted to bring our dog Copper as well, but the hospital wouldn't allow pets.

Finally, after two hours, Mum stopped breathing, and didn't start again. Chloe started to cry. Dad, his face gray, plopped into a chair and buried his face in his hand. As for me, my tears finally spilled over and my rage poured out.

"It's not fair!" I shouted. "Why did she have to die? What did she ever do wrong? She didn't deserve to die! She was going to live until she was a hundred and get a letter from the Queen!"

Chloe sniffed and wrapped her arms around me, holding me close as I cried and cried and cried. Dad joined in too and we stayed there, holding each other together.

That day I decided something. I never wanted to feel loss like this again. The memory still hurt just as much two years later. Chloe didn't understand. Loving was not worth the pain. If I cared about more people, then there was more chance I'd have to go through it all again. The hurt, the grief, the anger, and the overwhelming sadness. I had tried to stop caring, but I couldn't. So my only choice was to protect the people I already cared about and not care about anyone else. Then I could never hurt like that ever again.

When we got home, I swung my backpack over my shoulder and headed inside. Dad's car was absent, so I assumed he was still at work. Chloe followed me as we headed inside. There was an excited bark and our brown cocker-spaniel raced towards me, nearly knocking me off my feet. I laughed and reached down to stroke Copper's silky fur.

"Dinner will be ready for whenever Dad gets home," Chloe said, striding past me into the kitchen.

I nodded. "I'll be in my room." Racing down the hallway, I skidded into my room, with Copper at my heels. Kicking a couple of discarded items of clothing out of the way, I shut the door and plopped onto the carpet. My bag landed next to me. Copper sniffed my purple backpack as if he knew there was something unusual in it. Or as if he was planning to pee on it. Either one. I snatched the bag away, just in case it was the latter, and dug through it until I found the glass shoe. It was definitely solid glass. A glass high heeled shoe. I couldn't imagine it being very comfortable.

Placing the shoe on the floor in front of me, I stared at it. Where had it come from? Light sparkled on the shiny surface, reminding me vaguely of a picture in my memory. I leaned over to my bookshelf and yanked out my *Big Book of Fairytales*. Flipping through the pages, I landed on a page in Cinderella's story. The picture at the top of the page usually showed a glass slipper, just like the one I had on my bedroom floor. Now, instead of a shoe, the picture was of an empty staircase. My eyes flicked down the page to the writing. My mother had read me this book so many times when I was younger, that I nearly knew the words from memory. That's how I knew something was wrong.

"The prince raced after the princess, following her out to the grand staircase, but she was gone. The breeze blew. The trees seemed to sigh. All that was left was an empty staircase and a hollow feeling in the prince's heart," I read aloud.

Copper tilted his head to the side, as he often did when I read to him, and gave a tiny bark. It was almost like he knew that it wasn't right. I glanced back and forth between the book and the glass slipper. I double checked the book, just to make sure I hadn't imagined it, but it was clear as day. There was no slipper on the staircase, yet there was a slipper in my bedroom. What was going on? Could it be that the purple cloud had somehow transported the shoe from the Cinderella storybook? And if so, how was that even possible? It went against everything I had ever known. Stories were works of imagination, nothing more.

I slapped myself, just in case I had dreamed the whole thing and my body felt like waking up now, but the slipper was still there when I opened my eyes. So was the picture of the empty staircase. I tugged at my hair and moaned, utterly confused.

It was at that moment that the air in front of me started swirling purple. The cloud opened up as it had done in the forest and something large, fuzzy, and alive fell into my lap. I screamed.

CHAPTER TWO
What is Going On?

Whatever the thing was, it was warm and slightly squishy in my lap. After my initial fright, I gathered my strength and shoved the wriggling creature off me. It landed upside-down on the carpet, its many tiny legs wiggling in the air as it struggled to flip itself upright. Copper growled and sniffed it cautiously. I scrunched my legs up so it wouldn't touch me and observed the creature. It was about the same size as Copper, with a green body that appeared to be made of fuzzy green spheres, like large tennis balls stuck together, with a red sphere for its head. Finally, the thing managed to maneuver itself onto its feet and turned to blink at me. My heart sank as I recognized it from a book my mother had read to me and Chloe a very long time ago. The Hungry Caterpillar!

Suddenly I heard footsteps outside my door. Quick as a flash, I stuffed the glass slipper into my rubbish bin and shoved the caterpillar behind me. Chloe opened the door and stared at me.

"Cassie? Are you okay? I thought I heard you scream," she asked, frowning.

"No, I'm fine," I said, trying to contain the squirming caterpillar. "Maybe it was one of the kids next door?"

Chloe nodded. "Maybe. Well, Dad texted and said he'd be here soon. Have you started your homework?"

I rolled my eyes. "No."

"Do you want to invite a friend over tomorrow?" Chloe persisted.

I frowned. "If all you're going to do is try to talk me into things, you can leave." Chloe sighed, but left, closing the door behind her. As she did, I lost my grip on the caterpillar and he crawled out from behind me.

"Okay," I whispered. "Okay. So things from the fictional world are appearing around me. What is going on?"

I glanced at the caterpillar, who appeared to be chewing on the corner of my rubbish bin, then dug out the glass slipper and looked at it. Carefully, keeping an eye on the caterpillar, I reached over and slid my book, *The Hungry Caterpillar* , off the shelf. Of course I only kept it for sentimental reasons. Opening it, I knew immediately that something was wrong. The first page was blank. There was no picture, there were no words. I flicked through the whole book, but there was no caterpillar. Of course there wasn't. The Hungry Caterpillar was here, currently chewing on my failed attempt at a book report.

My eyes widened. Was he just going to keep eating and keep eating, like in the book? I gazed around, looking for a way to get rid of him. My gaze fastened on the window. At least it could eat green stuff outside. I yanked the window open, then turned back for the caterpillar. Picking him up, I it seemed like he was larger and heavier already. Puffing a little, I heaved him up and out through the window. My room faced the street, but we live on a quiet road, so I hoped nobody had seen. The caterpillar landed on his back and squirmed to his feet again. He gazed around, looking a little confused, then wandered off. I swiftly closed the window and pulled my curtains shut. This wasn't really happening. This couldn't be happening. What was going on?

"Cassie! Dinner time!" Chloe's shout came from the kitchen.

"Coming!" I called back.

Stuffing the glass slipper back into my bag, I zipped it shut, then headed out to the dining room.

"So how was school today?" Dad asked, when I plonked into my usual seat.

"Fine," I said. "We have a new group project for Maths starting on Monday."

"That's nice," Dad said. "So....who's in your group?"

"I'm asking to work alone," I told him. He already knew what the answer would be, I saw it on his face.

"How was work today?" Chloe asked Dad, changing the subject.

"Ah, well," Dad said eagerly, "I think we are getting closer! Just imagine it. Time travel!" Dad worked in a science research lab. They did all kinds of experiments with all kinds of things. Dad and a couple of his workmates were trying to unlock the secret of time travel. As far as I knew, all they had done so far was make an apple teleport from one room to the next. Not time travel, but definitely exciting.

"Got any plans for Saturday, Cass?" Chloe asked, knowing full well that there was no way I would.

"I'm going to take Copper out for a nice long walk," I told her. Copper, who was lying at my feet, hoping that some stray crumbs might fall into his mouth, perked up, his tail wagging.

"Is that it?" Chloe persisted. "Maybe you -"

I cut her off, "No, I don't want to invite a friend over. Friends are overrated." Chloe sighed, but didn't argue.

"Well, I thought maybe we could all go rock climbing at the Auckland Crag on Sunday," Dad suggested carefully, "Like we all used to do as a family."

A pang of grief sparked inside me and I wanted to refuse, but I forced myself to nod. I didn't want to hurt Dad's feelings. Besides, I loved rock climbing. So had Mum. I pulled my golden locket out from under my shirt and opened it to look at the picture inside. Dad, Mum, Chloe, and me, all smiling, all happy, all there. A tiny sliver of guilt wormed its way into my heart, at the thought of going climbing without Mum, but I ignored it. Mum was gone. As much as I wished she was here, she wasn't. I could only care about two people now: Dad and Chloe…. And Copper of course. I didn't need anyone else.

The next day I slept in until eleven like I always did on Saturdays. Chloe and Dad never complained. Dad worked on Saturdays, so he was gone by the time I headed out for breakfast.

"There was a news article this morning about a large caterpillar eating scooters and a bike stand," Chloe informed me as I sat down. She pointed to the newspaper on the table. "Have a read. It's really weird. I wouldn't have believed it, but multiple people say they have seen it."

I took a bite of my toast before glancing at the page. What I read nearly made me choke on my breakfast. When I had swallowed, I read it out loud so that Copper could hear.

"Multiple sightings of a large hungry caterpillar-like creature, rumored to be The Hungry

Caterpillar, have been reported. The chaos started in a small neighbourhood near the Port Hills when a lady spotted the caterpillar consuming an abandoned scooter. Another woman reported sighting the large green creature chewing up an entire bike stand. If you see this creature, please report it immediately. Do not go near it. We do not know how huge this caterpillar can grow and what it will eat. " When I had finished, Copper gave a small growl, as if he had understood everything and didn't like it.

"It was on the news too," Chloe said. "Apparently, it has a green body and a red head, just like the Hungry Caterpillar from the book Mum used to read to us when we were little."

"That's... weird," I said faintly. "I.....wonder where it came from?"

"That's not all," Chloe continued. "Apparently a woman discovered a large blind mouse in her back yard. Wearing clothes! It's so bizarre. I hope you'll be careful when you and Copper go walking later."

"Don't worry, Chloe," I assured her. "We will be. If I see a huge Hungry Caterpillar, I'll run the other way."

Chloe gave me a hint of a smile. I finished my breakfast and grabbed Copper's leash. He was very obedient and didn't really need the leash, but I felt like he was safer on it, so he couldn't go off too far. Copper led the way as we strode down the street and past a series of shops. I spotted some girls from my class, including Katelyn and Josie, but other than a small nod from Katelyn, they didn't acknowledge me.

Continuing until we reached the park, we stopped to play fetch. Strangely, after a few throws, Copper didn't go after the stick. He stopped suddenly, ears pricked up and he started growling softly.

"What's wrong, Cop?" I asked, walking towards him. He barked at what seemed to be empty air, staring at the sky above him. But a moment later, the sky was split by a bright purple light. A swirling purple cloud appeared four metres above the ground in the air over Copper's head. A small object fell out and the purple mass disappeared with a strange pop. No, not an object, another creature! It was black in colour and about the size and shape of a rugby ball, just furry and with arms and legs. Large purple eyes peered out above a tiny nose and mouth. The dark furry creature seemed a little disorientated for a moment, then its gaze fastened on me and it leapt up and dashed towards me.

"She coming! She coming!" the creature called in a grating warble. "Beware! Beware!"

"Who's coming?" I asked, incredulous and curious at the same time. I thought I might be imagining the funny little creature, but then it brushed against my leg and the coarse fur felt very real. Copper bounded over and sniffed it, perhaps thinking it might play with him.

"Danger! She coming!"

"Who? I don't know what you mean!" I said to the creature. "Where did you even come from?"

"She coming!" the creature cried. "Run!"

"Who? Who is coming?" I demanded, feeling strange and dizzy and ready to explode, as my mind processed this very strange encounter.

The creature finally seemed to hear me and stopped his frantic bouncing to look me in the eyes. "She power. She danger. She mystery. She -"

Abruptly, there was a flash of purple light and the creature was gone. Vanished. Not a trace was left. I could still feel remnants of the warmth of its fur on my leg, but it was gone. Thoroughly spooked, I glanced around to see if anyone else had seen, but there was no one around. I turned to Copper, who was growling softly, staring at the place the creature had been.

"Come on Cop," I said, my voice shaking a little, "Let's go home."

On the way home, my mind turned over the strange happenings and what the creature had said. Who was 'she'? Why was the creature so worried? Where did it even come from? As I walked, Copper trotted up ahead of me.

Suddenly, there was another purple flash just in front of me and the creature was back! Its purple eyes were wide and scared as it landed on the sidewalk and squeaked, "Danger!"

Copper came back and growled, apparently not appreciating its disappearing and reappearing act. I stared at it. It stared at me. It looked so scared. Cautiously, slowly, I reached out and picked up the trembling black form. I held it loosely, waiting for it to disappear. Instead, it just blinked at me. The street, only a little way from my house, seemed deserted, with an elderly woman being the only person in sight. I tucked the creature under my arm and ran the rest of the way home. Slamming the door behind me, I dashed to my room before Chloe could spot the strange little visitor. Then I placed it on the floor, maybe a little roughly. Again, it just blinked at me. Again it warbled, "Danger! Beware!"

I rolled my eyes. "I know. 'She coming.' Who even is she?"

The creature glanced at me with wide purple eyes. "Power! Danger!" it cried.

I double checked that I had shut my door, then faced the creature. "Okay, I get it. She danger," I told it, "You can be quiet about it." The creature snapped its mouth shut. I frowned. "So you understand me."

The creature gave what seemed to be a little nod, which looked strange on a creature that was really just a head with limbs attached. The little thing began waddling around in a circle, chasing after Copper's tail. He didn't seem dangerous, just a little dim. But he was the only being who had come through a portal so far who was able to speak, even if it was just 'Danger' and 'She coming,' so I was going to make the most of it.

"Okay, so... ground rules," I said, grabbing the creature by the arm and turning it so it faced me. "First of all, you don't leave my room, unless I permit you. Second, no shouting about danger or her coming or whatever, got it?"

The creature just stared at me. He, I decided to call him a he, gave me one slow blink, then nodded.

"Do you have a name?" I asked. I couldn't just keep calling him 'the creature.'

"Danger," the creature said.

"Your name is Danger?" I checked, a little surprised.

The creature gave another little bobbing nod. "Danger, Danger, Danger!" He started off his circling again.

"That's not very creative," I pointed out. Danger just gave a little bound and grasped the fur on Copper's tail with his three-fingered hand. Copper yelped and growled at him, but

Danger didn't seem bothered. I sighed. This was going to be interesting.

Abruptly, there was a knock on my door. Swift as a fox, I dumped a pile of dirty laundry over Danger, just as the door opened and Chloe peeked in.

"Oh, you are back," Chloe said. "I thought I heard you come in. I just wanted to remind you to get your climbing gear ready for tomorrow. We'll head out early in the morning, as soon as we're ready, to avoid the crowds."

"Alright," I said, pasting a cheerful grin on my face and hoping Chloe didn't notice the moving pile of laundry next to me. Chloe gave me a smile back and left. The door swung shut behind her. I dug Danger out of the pile of clothes and he waddled off across the floor towards Copper's bed. Copper growled and leaped after him, grabbing the creature's fur with his teeth.

"Copper, no!" I cried.

Copper, confused and slightly hurt, dropped Danger and trotted towards me, looking dejected. Danger was left sitting on the ground, his purple eyes fastened on me.

"Sorry Copper," I told Copper, "but you can't hurt him. He was just looking."

Copper gave me a look and settled down beside me. Danger glanced from Copper to me and back again. "Cop-pa," he said.

I stared at him. "What did you say?"

"Coppa," Danger repeated, "Coppa!" He said it more like cop-ah rather than cop-er, but I knew what he was saying.

"Coppa! Coppa!" Danger waddled in circles, waving his little hands in delight at the new word. It was hard not to smile.

Then it happened. One moment, Danger was dancing around, singing Copper's name, while Copper gave him an annoyed look, the next Danger was gone. Poof! Just like before. I was shocked, and reached out to where the little creature had been. He was gone. Nothing of him remained at all.

"Cassie! Dinner's ready!" Chloe's voice echoed down the hallway.

"I'm coming!" I called back somewhat shakily, my mind buzzing. I turned to Copper. "Come on."

As we left, I took one last glance at where Danger had been and thought I saw a spark of purple light. Then it was gone.

Chapter Three
Danger and Trouble

"Rise and shine, Sleeping Beauty!" My sheets were thrown back, revealing Chloe's grinning face above me. I yelped and tried to grasp the covers again as the cold air intruded into my warm world, but Chloe laughed and tugged me out of bed. "Come on, Cass! We're going rock climbing today, remember?"

I shook my head to let Chloe know that I didn't appreciate the early wake up call. She just smiled a sort of innocent smile.

"Fine," I muttered. I knew I would never win an argument not to go, so I shoved Chloe out of my room and quickly got changed. Heading out, I reminded Dad to grab his old climbing belt, before wolfing down some breakfast. As soon as I had finished eating, Chloe whirled in and plopped my bowl in the sink, then dragged me out to the hall. I barely had time to grab all my things before the three of us were in the car and driving to Auckland Crag, a rock climbing crag in the Port Hills.

While Dad and Chloe chatted in the front, I zoned out and daydreamed about random fictional events. When I heard the words 'fictional creatures' though, I tuned into the conversation.

"Martin said that his wife found a strange little bearded man in their kitchen," Dad was saying, "This little man was only the size of a child, but he had a long white beard and a strange little floppy hat. She fainted away at the sight of him and when she awoke, he had disappeared. I don't think anyone would have believed her before we heard about that large caterpillar creature."

"It is so strange," Chloe said. "Could he have been one of the dwarfs, do you think? From Snow White?"

"However would that be possible?" Dad responded.

Chloe shrugged, keeping her eyes on the road. "The same way the Hungry Caterpillar could find its way here, I guess."

At that moment, I was distracted by a purple flash at the corner of my vision. I turned hurriedly to see a little furry rugby ball land on the seat beside me. It was Danger. Again. My eyes widened.

"Dange-" he started.

I swiftly grabbed him and stuffed him into my backpack, muffling his cries. Dad turned to look at me.

"Did you hear that? I thought I just heard somebody say danger."

I shrugged. "We did just pass the skate-park. Maybe one of those kids shouted it."

Dad frowned. "Perhaps. It sounded like it was in the car." He looked around the back seat then turned back to his conversation with Chloe.

I opened my bag and peered in to find Danger staring back at me, his purple eyes wide.

"You are in so much trouble," I whispered in my softest whisper, "Be quiet."

Once we had reached the start of the trail leading to the crag, Chloe took the lead. It gave me a little pang of grief to see her leading, just like Mum used to. Dad followed Chloe, carrying the ropes and other gear, and I brought up the rear, with Danger trailing behind me. I had let him out of my bag, hoping he would have enough sense to hide if Dad or Chloe turned around. Hanging back, I let Chloe and Dad get a decent lead on their way up the hill. Once they were out of sight, Danger glanced at me.

"Coppa?" he asked.

"Copper isn't here," I said.

"Danger!" Danger said. "Beware! She coming!"

Frustrated, I gritted my teeth together and nudged the little creature along with my foot.

He seemed to get the message and was soon prancing up the track ahead of me chanting 'Coppa' and 'Danger.' I hoped that Chloe and Dad were far enough ahead that they wouldn't hear.

Who was coming, though? Danger seemed frightened of whoever she was. What was going on? The glass slipper, the Hungry Caterpillar, the dwarf, Danger… were they all related somehow? They all had one thing in common, all except Danger. The slipper, the caterpillar, and the dwarf were all from well known fiction stories. Danger, he was different.

"Unless…" I mumbled out loud. "What if his story just isn't a well known one?"

"Danger! Danger!" came the cry as Danger tumbled past me, rolling face over feet down the hill. It was a rather comical sight that would have had me doubled over laughing at any other time. But not now. Not with a mystery afoot.

"Danger!" I shouted as loud as I dared. "Get back here!"

Once Danger had caught up with me again, I let him follow me up to the crag, where Chloe and Dad were waiting. Danger seemed to sense that he shouldn't be spotted and he slipped away into the trees.

"There you are!" Chloe exclaimed, her eyes lighting up and her frown lifting. "We were getting worried!"

"Yeah, sorry, I was just... uh... distracted by... the birds," I fumbled with the excuse.

Chloe gave me a strange look, but she must have been too excited to be on a family outing to complain that I was acting weird.

We set up the ropes and our gear and took turns belaying each other up the climbs. I had been rock climbing at a rock climbing gym with my mum since I was six years old. I continued to go every week, even though it wasn't the same without her. As much as my mother had loved the climbing gym, she had always said that there was nothing better than a cliff face and a top-rope. I agreed with her. Outside, the sun shone down and the breeze ruffled my hair and I felt free.

Just as the sun was beginning to disappear behind the hills, I spotted a swirling purple cloud mass appear on the rock face, a little way along from where we had been climbing. It was gradually growing wider. A sinking feeling settled inside me as I wondered what would appear next. But unlike the other times the cloud just kept growing.

"Woah, what's that?" Chloe asked from where she was coiling the ropes.

Amazed, Dad stepped forward to examine the purple roiling cloud, but I held out my arm to stop him. Fortunate, as just then, there was a bright flash of light and a female figure appeared out of the portal. The three of us instinctively pressed ourselves against the rock face as the woman's robe settled around her legs.

She was a tall woman, with wavy gray hair and gray eyes. Her green robe brushed the purple cloud she stood on, which somehow seemed to hover in midair, and she held a long wooden staff. At the staff's tip was an orb of swirling purple. The woman gave a truly evil cackle and without even looking around, began to speak in a rough voice.

"I am Glorathy Dodge, most powerful sorceress of all! Fear me puny humans! I have been overlooked and neglected long enough. Now I will be seen! You have ignored my story, passed it up for others, but that will stop now! Now, I will have my revenge! You humans have no power! You have ignored me at your peril! I have grown so powerful that I have created hundreds of thousands of portals between all the different story worlds, and this portal," she threw her hands wide, "connects the fictional world to your world! You will all perish! Overrun, and over powered! " Glorathy Dodge raised her staff dramatically and lightning struck the tip. Then she paused and looked around. Her view of us was blocked by a slight outcropping of rocks.

"Oh buckets!" Glorathy growled. "Curse you, you stupid staff! There's no one here! I wanted Auckland, not a puny pile of rocks in the middle of nowhere!"

I risked a peek around the rock and saw her bashing her staff on the ground.

"I must figure out where I went wrong," Glorathy muttered, appearing to be speaking to herself. "I was sure I had all the kinks ironed out. I'll have to make my entrance somewhere else instead. I was so sure that would work! Oh buckets, oh-" Her voice was cut off as she flew her cloud back into the portal and vanished. But the portal didn't. In the now dimming light, the cloudy portal glowed with an ethereal purple light. And it was still growing.

"That doesn't seem... good," Chloe whispered, looking shaken.

"We need to get out of here," I said, my brain switching into protective mode.

"But- How did she-" Dad faltered, glancing at the portal. I could practically see the drool and hear the cogs turning. "The secret of inter-dimensional travel," Dad murmured, "it could all be contained in that... whatever it is."

"We can come back tomorrow," Chloe assured him. "You can bring some test equipment."

Dad nodded, even though I was shaking my head.

"We should call the police," I protested.

"Not yet!" Dad said quicly, "If they come, they'll block everything off. I need to study it first! It's a once in a lifetime opportunity!"

Chloe looked uncertain but she nodded. I didn't say anything. There was no way Dad or Chloe were returning, even if I had to restrain them myself.

Morning came and I woke up to hear Dad digging through the hallway cupboard right outside my door.

"Where is it?" I heard him mutter.

Copper, lying on my feet, stirred as I shifted in bed. He opened one chocolate brown eye to look at me. As he did, my door banged open. Chloe stood there. My eyes widened in surprise, because Chloe always lectured me about not slamming doors. She grinned at me.

"We're going on an adventure, Cass! Dad wants to examine that cloudy portal thing!"

I groaned, the events of yesterday crawling back into my tired brain. "No. We can't go there. You heard what the crazy lady with the staff said. She's a wacko. We should just tell the police and let them handle it."

Dad appeared behind Chloe, "This could be the secret to inter-dimensional travel, Cassie. Think about it! That would be amazing. We will tell the authorities, but let me get a good look at it first. That strange lady was wanting to go to Auckland anyway. She won't be back to our pile of rocks!" His eyes were lit up and his hands moved quickly, trying to get me to visualize inter-dimensional travel.

I gave them both a skeptical look, "You guys both have work and I have school. We can't."

"Already called the school," Chloe said, smiling. "Dad and I both took the day off work! No getting out of this one, Cass! Come on! Copper can come too!"

Copper, hearing his name, perked up and gave me a longing look.

"Alright," I muttered grumpily, flipping my covers back, "But if it looks dangerous, we're getting out of there."

"Of course, of course," Dad said, waving a hand dismissively. His eyes still held that dreamy look. "Don't you worry."

Copper pranced ahead of me as I followed Chloe and Dad up the hill and back to the rock-face. When we arrived, I stopped short. The portal was at least the size of an overgrown elephant, circular and pulsating. Dad approached it without fear and began taking measurements with his tape measure, and other gadgets. He didn't even seem to notice that the very ground he stood on had changed.

Luscious green moss coated the rock face around the portal and the stony ground below it. Little pink fluorescent mushrooms sprouted among the dense clumps of greenery. A trickle of water had sprung from somewhere inside the portal and now dribbled down the hill past where the trail came out. Occasional sparkles appeared here and there around a patch of small yellow daisies, but they moved too fast for me to see properly what they were.

"This is… different," I said, stepping forward with caution.

"It's beautiful," Chloe whispered, her eyes scanning the moss, the mushrooms, and the delicate yellow flowers.

Flash! Something dropped out of the portal and landed on the mossy ground below.

Whatever the something was, it didn't seem to appreciate its not so soft landing.

"Slithering slitherboats!" came a gruff voice, as the thing struggled to maneuver itself upright. When it did, I couldn't help gasping. It looked a little like Danger. The shape of its body was the same, only this creature had a long neck and a small giraffe-like head. It had pale gray fur and huge orange eyes. A soft fluffy tail, like that of a squirrel, sprouted from its behind, brushing the ground.

"H-hello?" Chloe stuttered, her eyes almost as huge as the giraffe creature's.

The creature's head swiveled around to look at Chloe and I. "Ah! Dimming dinklebots! What're ya doin' there? Tryna scare the life outta a poor ol' Ruggle like me, eh?"

"Oh, uh..... no," Chloe said hurriedly. "Not at all. We just... well..."

"You just popped out of that portal thing," I finished, pointing to the large purple cloud.

The long neck swiveled around to look up at the portal, then turned back to us. "So I must've, eh? Was one jolly ol' time of a ride! Ain't ever seen enathin' like it afore."

"This might seem weird," I began, aware that Chloe was watching me, "but do you know a little creature called Danger? He looks a little like you, only… shorter. "

"Ya betcha dinglehops, I do!" the creature said, nodding his head. "He be me mate from back 'ome! Keeps disappearin' now like. Can't seem t' find 'im enawhere."

"Oh," I said, my brain struggling to process the jumbled, broken speech.

"Me name's Trouble, by the way!" the creature said. "Jus' if you do be needin' me someday! Ima need ta go find me mate Danger now! Gimme a shout, enatime, an' I'll be there! If I can hear ya like!" Trouble turned towards the trees and waddled off, as we stood there, dumbfounded. His long neck seeming to make him even more comical than Danger.

At the last second before he disappeared into the undergrowth, Trouble swerved to look directly at us. "Be ceerful round dat portal, like," he said, suddenly sounding grave. "She's coming. And this place ain't never goin' be ready for 'er." He swiveled back and headed off into the woods.

Chloe turned to look at me sternly. "You've seen something like that thing before and didn't tell us?"

"It doesn't matter," I said, staring down at my feet.

"I think it does," Chloe said. By the way she said it, I could tell there was some serious eyebrow raising and arm folding going on.

Dad on the other hand was so enthralled with the portal, he didn't even seem to have noticed the appearance of Trouble. He was muttering to himself as he poked at the cloudy surrounds of the portal.

"Careful Dad," Chloe said. She didn't try and pull him away though.

"You heard Trouble!" I looked at Chloe like she was crazy. "We have to get out of here! That witch lady might come back!"

"Witch?!" came an indignant screech. There was a flash of purple light brighter than any before and I shielded my eyes. When the light had faded enough that I could see, I found myself staring at the imposing, if not slightly strange, figure of Glorathy Dodge. Her gray eyes were smoldering as she looked me up and down.

"I'll have you know that I'm no stinking witch!" she growled. "I'm a sorceress! The most powerful sorceress in all of the worlds!"

"Witches and sorceresses don't exist," Chloe said. "Neither does magic."

I stared at Chloe, sure my eyes were about to pop out of my head with disbelief. How could she not believe what was right in front of her very eyeballs? Did she think there was a scientific explanation for all this?

"Don't exist?" Glorathy cackled. "That's a laugh! How many stories about wicked witches have you read, girl? All of those witches are real!"

Chloe frowned, the logical side of her brain clearly taking over. "But stories are just works of imagination, made up in someone's mind and put on paper."

"Works of imagination?" Glorathy screeched. "Made up?"

"Everything can be explained by science," Dad suddenly broke into the conversation.

I gritted my teeth. What were they trying to do? Make the lady with the powers mad? What good would that do?

"Pah, science!" Glorathy snorted with contempt. "What can it do? Magic is the real source of power."

"Magic is just tricks of the mind," Dad told Glorathy. "Even what we think of as magic can be explained by science."

I gaped at my family, unable to believe they were trying to convince a magical storybook villain that magic wasn't real and that she was just a part of someone's imagination.

"Tricks of the mind?" Glorathy shouted. "Science? This world is the dumbest I've ever been to!" She paused for a breath. "That's it! I've had enough of being ridiculed! I'll show you tricks of the mind!"

With a swish of her staff two purple-toned clouds appeared and shoved my family towards the portal. I watched, horrified, my feet seemingly stuck to the ground. "No!" I cried.

Just as Glorathy was about to fly back through the swirling purple wormhole, she turned back and winked at me. "I do love a good bit of hide and seek! See you on the other side, girl."

Then they were gone. Copper growled and darted up to the portal, sniffing it. I just felt numb. Gone. They were gone! I reran the whole thing over in my head. I should have stopped Glorathy, saved Chloe and Dad, gotten them away safely. My brain stalled on Glorathy's final words.

I do love a good bit of hide and seek! See you on the other side...

Was I supposed to follow her? Was that how I got my family back? "I don't really see another way," I murmured. "What do you think, Cop?"

Copper just glanced at me and wagged his tail. Picking him up, I clambered up to the portal.

"I'm coming Dad! I'm coming Chloe!" I called.

Then I fell into the purple wormhole.

CHAPTER FOUR
Which Witch?

I got the feeling I was falling, although I also felt as if I was standing still. Images seemed to drift by through the purple void I was floating in. It was like a long, straight tunnel stretching down into nothingness. Wind whipped around me as the pictures began moving faster, the wild breeze flinging my hair into my face. Spitting out the wavy locks, I tried to keep track of my surroundings. Where was Glorathy? Where were Chloe and Dad? I tightened my hold on Copper as the images whirled past even faster.

My gaze fastened on an image of an elegant princess holding the hand of a handsome prince. It whizzed past so quickly I only got a glimpse. The next picture that caught my eye was a pair of gray haired pirates lying face-down on a boat, seemingly dead, but who knew. Another image caught my eye. It looked like Danger and Trouble, standing in front of a dark bridge over black water. More and more pictures flew past. A wiry-haired witch with a crooked nose, a towering beanstalk, a burning city, a two-headed dragon flying over a mountainside, a beautiful girl in a glass case, a ragged boy riding on the back of an ostrich. The snapshots of countless stories whizzed past.

Suddenly, I fell, for real this time. Tumbling, toppling, plummeting into a deep purple abyss. Glorathy's familiar cackle filled my ears as my vision faded to black.

A hard surface pressed against my spine. Where was I? Blinking my eyes open, I gazed upward. The sun blazed down on me, out of a sky that was as blue as the bluebirds chirping in the trees around me. No clouds showed in the clear sky. I lifted my head to find myself spreadeagled on the rough ground. Sitting up, I pulled my hoodie over my head and tied it around my waist. Wherever I had ended up, it was way warmer than back home. A frown formed on my lips when I got a better look at the material I was sitting on. The ground underneath me was paved with yellow bricks. The road led off in two different directions, glittering in the sun.

"A yellow brick road..." I murmured. "No way..." Copper squirmed in my arms and I released him cautiously. He sniffed the yellow path suspiciously and gave a little bark. Some of the bluebirds fluttered away from the trees nearby, tweeting crossly, but nothing else stirred. There was no way this was real. It was one thing to have fictional characters in the real world. But it seemed now *I* was in the *fictional world*.

"We're in the Wizard of Oz," I whispered. Copper barked as if in agreement.

How could we get out of here? And where was Glorathy? What was she doing to Chloe and Dad? How was I going to find them?

Copper pranced off along the yellow brick road in one direction. With no real reason for making another choice, I decided to follow. The whole time, the cogs in my brain were turning rapidly, trying to figure out what to do, how to get out of this story. How to find my family. I probably needed to find another one of those purple portals. Glorathy had mentioned that all the fictional worlds were connected through portals. If a portal brought me here, a portal could get me out.

"Alright, Copper," I said, glancing at the silky brown puppy, "Lead us out of here."

Copper bounded along, with me running behind him. There was nobody else on the road. Our surroundings consisted of only grass and a few trees. I vaguely wondered what part of the story we were in. Was Dorothy making her way along the yellow brick road to find the Wizard of Oz? Or was she already at the Emerald City? I guess it didn't really matter.

As we continued along the path, the trees on either side thickened and we soon entered a forest. "Reckon this is where Dorothy meets the lion?" I said to Copper. I frowned. "Or was it the Tin Man?" It had been a long time since I'd read the Wizard of Oz.

Copper gave me a look, as if to tell me he didn't know or it didn't matter, then headed off to sniff the roots of a nearby tree. As he did, there was a flash and a pop. A gray-haired lady in a pointy hat appeared, hovering in mid air. For a moment I thought she might be Glorathy, but she was much too short. She held a crooked wand instead of a staff and the end sparked a little.

"Um..." I said uncertainly. "Who are you?"

The woman cackled, "I am the Wicked Witch of the Compass!"

I frowned, confused. "Uh..."

"Like the Wicked Witch of the West, or the East, or the North, or the South," the witch huffed. "Honestly, why does nobody ever get that?"

"Um... okay... so, did you....want something?" I said, glancing around, trying to look at anything but the large wart on the witch's equally large nose, which was wobbling around as she spoke.

"Want something?" the witch scoffed, "From you?" She landed on the ground and doubled over with laughter, as if it was the funniest idea in the world.

Copper took that moment to wander over and sniff the witch's pointed boots. Then, before I could do anything about it, he lifted his leg and did his business right there on her foot! I had to stifle a giggle. The witch screeched in disgust.

"Revolting creature!" the witch screamed. "My best boots! My mother will be so disappointed in me! I promised I'd keep them clean till Tuesday! I'll get you for that!"

She flicked her wand and Copper flew into her spindly arms. As soon as her knobbly fingers closed around him, he turned rigid in her grasp. She turned to me.

"You come too, girl," she said with a yellow-toothed grin, "I always have room for another snack."

I felt myself freeze in place. My limbs stiffened and I was lifted off the ground by some unseen force. Then we were speeding over the land below, heading for the mountains in the distance.

The witch, who apparently didn't even ride a broomstick like witches did in most stories, floated gently into a damp, dimly lit cave, with craggy outcrops of rock jutting from the floor at the entrance, making it look like a large mouth. With a wave of her sparking wand, my frozen form followed her in, hitting the side of a rocky clump on the way. Literally unable to make a noise, I settled for yelping inwardly.

The witch kicked at a lump in the floor and cursed when nothing happened. "Dinglehoops! I really need to get someone in to look at my lighting. I'm sure that this is happening more and more often," she muttered the last part under her breath. She kicked the rock again, more aggressively this time. There was a pause. Almost reluctantly, light flickered into the cave from an unknown source, illuminating nearly the whole cave, leaving only a few dark cracks and crevices.

"That's better!" the Wicked Witch of the Compass exclaimed. She glanced over at me. Her purple eyes narrowed in her sharp-chinned little face. "Where to put you…" she mumbled.

With a flick of her wand, I gained control of my limbs again and dropped onto the floor. Before I could think about running, or even rubbing my sore bottom, a glass box appeared around me, barely tall enough for me to stand up in. The witch cackled, clapping her hands together and dropping Copper onto the stony floor in the process. Copper raced over to me, pawing the glass and whining.

"Shut up, you infernal beast!" the witch hissed. "Now, where did I put that…" she wandered off.

I took the time to get my breath back, stand up, and gaze around. The walls were just cave walls, jagged rocks, with moss growing in some places. There was apparently a leak somewhere far above, because water dripped down from the roof and landed in a purple plastic bucket placed strategically underneath.

"This is your secret witch base?" I said to the witch when she returned. She turned when she heard me, and raised an eyebrow. She huffed, placing her hands on her hips. "It's low budget! I spent most of it on the lights."

I couldn't help a smirk. "Don't you have magic? Can't you just magic up lights and carpets and nice things, like no leaks?"

The witch gave a growling snort and turned away from me to keep searching for something.

"Can't witches magic up things?" I persisted.

The witch finally found what she wanted, a large oven, and used her magic to float it behind her as she strode over to me. Her face was red with anger.

"I am a proper witch!" she insisted. "I am just as wicked as my sisters were!"

I frowned. "Honestly, you don't seem to be able to do much. Wouldn't you have more fancy witch stuff if you were a real witch? Wouldn't you have some friends, or maybe some servants?"

The witch looked ready to explode. "I am a real witch! I'm powerful! I don't need friends! Friends are for the weak!"

I could tell I'd hit a sore spot.

"Why don't you stop talking, girl?" the witch said, zipping over to poke a finger at the glass. "I will do with you what I want."

I sensed that she meant it. Hauling her little black potbellied stove over so that it was next to my glass cage, the witch muttered an incantation, pointing her wand at the oven. Sparks flew but nothing else happened.

"Buckets of doodlerats!" the witch cursed. She tried again. This time a small fire lit in the oven. The witch grinned and clapped her hands joyously. Hurrying away, she rummaged through something just out of my view and came back with a cardboard box and a large black pot. She placed the pot on the stove and gestured to it with her wand. Water appeared and started bubbling immediately. The witch looked pleased with herself.

"Are you really going to cook me?" I said, suddenly the tiniest bit frightened of this wannabe witch.

The witch snorted with laughter. "No, girl, of course not! My cousin ate children! Dreadful habit. I tried once, but they taste disgusting! Horrible! Not at all as sweet as they act!" She chuckled. "I'm making soup."

Reaching into her box, she pulled out a couple of carrots and tossed them into her pot. I gazed around again, glad that the threat of being cooked alive was gone. I needed a way to get out of here. Who knew what Glorathy was doing to my family right now?

"Why are you a wicked witch?" I asked abruptly, turning to look back at the witch, who was tasting her carrot soup.

"What?" the witch gave me a quizzical look.

"You heard me," I said, gesturing to her wand. "Why are you a 'wicked' witch? Why not a nice witch?"

"Well," the witch spluttered, "I- that is- my sisters were wicked witches, so I am also a wicked witch. I will be the most wicked of them all. I will be known far and wide. The Wicked Witch of the Compass!"

Copper barked. The witch glared at him. "Stop mocking me, vermin!"

"You seem pretty lonely," I pressed onward. "If you were a nice witch, you could help the townspeople, just like the Witches of the North and South. You'd have lots of friends and get to use your magic."

The witch stopped stirring her soup and looked slightly thoughtful. Her eyes suddenly lit up. "I've had an idea, girl! What if I was a nice witch? I could help the townspeople! And use magic!"

I barely suppressed an eye-roll.

"That's it! That's what I'll do! I'll go talk to the Munchkins right now!" Ignoring me completely, she abandoned her soup and zoomed out of the cave. Once she was gone, the lights flickered and faded, the soup stopped boiling, the two carrots clunked to the bottom of the pot, and my cage disappeared. Copper barked excitedly and I stroked his silky fur.

"Alright, Copper," I said. "Let's find a portal." I glanced towards the exit. I genuinely hoped that the 'Wicked Witch of the Compass' could find some friends and help some people. As much as she wanted me to believe it, the witch didn't seem very wicked.

Copper barked again and brushed against my leg. I glanced down, meeting his dark brown gaze.

"What is it, Cop?" I asked. He woofed again and pattered a small distance away, deeper into the cave. I hesitated and Copper turned back to me and barked loudly, as if annoyed.

"Okay, I'm coming!" I said. I followed him around the corner and there, embedded in the stone wall, was a portal, not unlike the one in the climbing crag in the Port Hills. This portal was smaller, only just large enough for me to fit through. There was a problem though.

"That's weird," I said, shaking my head. "That witch is a strange person."

Random boards and pieces of metal had been tacked up over the portal, as if the witch had tried to get rid of it. It hadn't worked. Copper sniffed the portal and barked again.

"Yes, yes," I said, rolling my eyes. "You're so smart Copper. Well done."

Copper pranced in a circle while I tried to find a place to break through the boards. It seemed that the witch had used a mix of glue and nails to stick the planks and metal there. I wandered over to the witch's large chest and dug out the nearest utensil – a metal fork. I also discovered some rope that I rolled up tight and tucked into my pocket in case I needed it later. Using the fork, I pried off some of the boards. Just enough to create a gap I could fit through.

"Ready, Copper?" I said. I clutched my fork like a weapon and picked Copper up with my other arm. Cautiously, I poked one foot through the swirling edge of the hole. A strange sensation covered my leg, sort of tingly and numb at the same time. I ducked and slid my other leg through. Holding my breath, I let myself drop into the portal wormhole.

I felt myself falling again, just as before. A breeze picked up. I was plummeting towards a purple void as images flew past. Just like last time, I managed to get a look at the pictures. The same ones actually. Only this time, instead of a wiry-haired witch cackling nastily, the witch was accompanied by several townspeople and they appeared to be trying to fix a well, all working together. I barely had time to smile at the scene before the pictures started moving faster.

And there were the pictures I somehow couldn't miss, seeming to impress themselves on my mind. A towering beanstalk, a burning city, a two-headed dragon flying over a mountainside, a beautiful girl in a glass case, a ragged boy riding on the back of an ostrich.

"One down," the whispery voice of Glorathy said, an edge of sarcasm to her voice, "Five to go… good luck Cassie."

Then the images flew faster and I fell and fell and fell until everything went black.

CHAPTER FIVE
Allies?

Oof! I landed harder this time, knocking the breath out of me. Copper wriggled out of my arms and I heard him pattering around, sniffing. My eyes snapped open and I bolted upright, realizing that I might not necessarily be in a safe place.

Around me was a garden. The grass was green and lush and the trees bowed over the ground like they were worshiping it, providing shade for anyone in the yard. A fence surrounded the garden. Peeling paint and knotholes riddled the white pickets. One side of the garden was bordered by a small cottage. Leaning up against the cottage was a cow. She was an old cow, with a black and white pelt and large docile eyes. Only her mouth and tail moved as she chewed her cud.

Glancing around, I realized I was OK. Nobody could see me or where I'd come from. The portal was gone and I was sitting alone, except for the cow. Copper bounded over to the cow and gave a woof. Surprisingly the cow didn't seem bothered.

"What story are we in this time?" I whispered softly, unsure if anyone was nearby. "Are we even in another story?" Copper looked over at me but didn't make a sound as he went back to exploring the garden. The cow kept chewing her cud.

I stood up and wandered over to the gate. It creaked as I opened it. Giving a short sharp bark, Copper bounded over and followed me out. I shut the gate behind me, hoping nobody had seen. Hearing footsteps, I quickly grabbed Copper and ducked behind a nearby bush. A boy about my age with tousled brown hair, who was wearing ragged clothes and had a dirty face, came around the corner of the cottage and stepped right up to the fence.

I held my breath. If he looked over towards us, we were caught. Luckily, the boy just frowned and stared over the fence at the cow.

"Weird," he muttered, "I thought I heard a dog barking." He looked at the cow. "Did you hear it, Daisy?"

By the sound of it, the cow just kept chewing her cud. I couldn't help but stifle a giggle that this boy was talking to his cow. The boy shrugged, turned around, and walked back towards the cotage. Before he got there, there was the sound of a door creaking open and a woman's voice called out.

"Jack! This is the third morning in a row that Daisy hasn't given any milk! This is happening too often. It's time to take her to the market to be sold!"

"But-" muttered the boy, Jack.

"No buts!" the woman I assumed was his mother called back. "We need the money. I'm sorry, Jack."

Then the door slammed shut. Jack sighed.

I peeked through the bush. After he had attached a leash to Daisy's neck, he opened the gate and led her out. "Come on, Daisy," Jack said, a trace of sadness in his voice. "Let's get you to the market."

He and the cow slowly plodded away. With a glance at the house, then back at the boy, I cautiously rose up and followed them. I knew what story I was in now.

I had no trouble keeping up with Jack and Daisy. Even though I knew what was meant to happen, I was curious to see when Jack was confronted by the man who would sell him the magic beans.

"I'm sorry Daisy," Jack told his cow.

I suppressed a giggle at how ridiculous it was to talk to a cow. Copper gave me a look.

Jack stopped. I glanced ahead and saw that a funny little man with a long gray beard and a straw hat was pushing a four-wheeled wagon along the road towards us. The traces at the front were empty, which explained why he was pushing it. The wagon was covered with a blanket, so I couldn't tell what was inside.

When his wagon was level with Daisy and Jack, the little man halted and turned to look at the cow. He was even shorter up close, maybe even shorter than the Wicked Witch of the Compass had been. It was a miracle he could even see over his own wagon.

"Hello there young man," the old man croaked, looking up at Jack.

"Hello," Jack replied in a tone that sounded like he didn't want to talk to the man.

"That's a fine cow you have there," the man continued, eyeing Daisy.

"I'm taking her to the market to sell her," Jack told the man sullenly.

"I'll buy her from you," the little man said eagerly, "I need a cow to pull my wagon."

"How much are you offering?" Jack asked.

"Well," the man said, digging in the pockets of his dirty dungarees, "I don't have any money, but I've got some magic beans." The man produced a handful of pale green beans.

I thought I knew the story of Jack and the Beanstalk. I had always thought that Jack was pretty stupid to trade his cow for some beans. So what happened next shocked me.

Jack snorted. "Beans? Are you kidding me?" he swatted the beans out of the man's hand and onto the ground. Neither of the two were looking at the beans as they landed, but I was. The beans evaporated.

"Hey!" the man yelled, "Those were perfectly good beans!"

Jack sighed. "Come on, Daisy, let's go home."

Surprised by his change of mind, I barely had time to dive into the bushes before Jack turned and led Daisy back the way he had come. The man grumbled something about kids having no manners, then got back behind his wagon and started heading after Jack. He turned down a side road a little further down.

I dragged my gaze over to where the beans had fallen. I knew the story. I knew what would happen.

"Keep an eye out for people Copper," I said, looking around for a place to hide, "We're staying here tonight."

I could somehow sense that Glorathy wasn't in this world, so I had to find another portal. And if I knew anything about super cliche 'bad guys,' Glorathy would want to make this as hard as possible. Which meant my portal was up in the clouds.

I must have nodded off because when I opened my eyes, it was morning. And that was not all. A huge beanstalk, as thick as a house and taller than the trees, had sprouted overnight, just like in the story. I quickly hurried over and examined the stalk. It had one main stem, with many other vine-like ones twining around it. Leaves branched out at some points, but other than that it wound straight up into the sky.

Hearing a voice behind me, I whirled around. It was Jack. His head was down and he muttered to himself.

"Apologize to the funny little man? He should apologize to me! I shouldn't have told Mum th-" Jack's voice abruptly broke off, because he had spotted me. There was nowhere for me to hide. He was staring at me, confused.

"Um..." I said. "Hi?"

Jack frowned. "Who are you? And why do you have blue hair?"

"I'm Cassie," I began, then realized what he'd said. "Wait, what?!" I yanked the end of my ponytail around in front of me and stared at it in horror. My normally golden brown hair was now a brilliant ocean blue colour. I gritted my teeth. "That witch!" I muttered.

Jack, meanwhile, was eyeing the beanstalk behind me in amazement. "Were you going to climb that?"

I shrugged. "Yeah."

Jack squinted at me, as if wondering why the strange girl with blue hair and weird clothes was planning on climbing the giant green column that had appeared out of nowhere.

"Listen Jack-" I tried.

"How do you know my name?" Jack asked, eyes narrowed.

"Uh… oh, nuts," I muttered, realizing I had just fallen deeper into the hole I had dug for myself.

"Is that a….beanstalk?" Jack asked suddenly.

I realized that his eyes had widened and now he stared at the huge stalk behind me. I shrugged and nodded, then blurted out, "It's your story. You're supposed to know this stuff."

"Story?" Jack asked. The confusion in his eyes was as evident as an elephant in a pig pen. What could I say now? If I told him the truth, he would either think I was crazy, or I would ruin his story.

"Like… a book," I said. That was really stupid.

"You're saying that I'm... in a book?" Jack said. Skepticism was written all over his face. He didn't believe me.

"Yeah," I plowed onward. "Jack and the Beanstalk." My finger poked the beanstalk beside me. "Beanstalk," then I pointed at him, "and Jack."

"I have my own book?" Jack asked. If his eyes got any wider, they would fall out of his head.

"Oh, nuts, what have I gotten myself into," I muttered under my breath. "Look Jack, I'd love to stay and chat-" that was a blatant lie "-but I really have to go and save my family from an evil sorceress."

"An evil sorceress?" Jack repeated. He squinted at me, as if he wasn't quite sure I was real. "You're... serious right now?"

I shrugged and nodded.

"This evil sorceress is probably rich, right? With gold?" Jack murmured speculatively, almost to himself.

I frowned, unsure what he was getting at.

"I'll accompany you," Jack said decisively, "To save your family I mean. In return, I get any gold we find, to help my mother."

I snorted. "Uh, I don't think so. I don't do freeloader friends, alright? If you want gold, go find your own. I am going to get my family back. By myself!"

Jack crossed his arms and glared at me, "You can't stop me. Plus, you're a girl, I can't let you go alone. You wouldn't make it very far anyway."

"Wanna bet?" I retorted. I called Copper to me and used the rope I had taken from the witch to make a harness and tie him onto my back. Jack looked on with curiosity. Once I was sure Copper was secure, I started climbing.

I had climbed with Copper on my back before. It had been part of the training that I had set for myself. Admittedly the harness had been better. Being a small cocker spaniel though,

Copper wasn't extremely heavy, so I only had to adjust a little for the extra weight.

As I started to climb, I was aware that there was no safety net or rope or anything up here. If I fell, I would die. Luckily, the beanstalk was riddled with little handholds and footholds that I could dig my fingers and toes into. Copper stayed silent as I scrambled upwards, sensing my tension. There were terrifying, death-defying moments where one of my hands or feet slipped, one time I dangled with one hand over the ground below, but I managed to pull myself back up.

After climbing for maybe half an hour, I dragged myself up onto what seemed like clouds with exhausted, trembling arms. There was a moment where I was worried I would just fall right through the clouds, but here the clouds were more solid. Just a little springy. I released Copper from his bonds before flopping down onto the white surface, breathing hard. Copper stared down at me with a certain look that seemed to be my punishment for making him endure the climb, before he wandered away to explore.

"Don't go far," I panted. Copper just barked.

Sitting up, I gazed around. The fluffy cloud area faded into luscious grass a little way away. A castle loomed in the distance. I vaguely wondered if that was where Jack was supposed to get his golden goose.

There was a groan from behind me and I whipped my head around to see Jack hauling himself up onto the cloud.

"Did you follow me?" I said, glaring at him. Which seemed a stupid question, as it was obvious, but somehow I wasn't thinking straight.

"No!" Jack protested, sounding even more out of breath than I was, as he plonked himself down on the soft white surface. He clearly wasn't used to pacing himself while climbing.

I gave him a pointed look, one that I hoped said 'Then why are you here?'

Jack sighed. "Fine, so I followed you, hoping to work together. You have to admit, people are always stronger with allies. That's what we are – allies. Not friends, alright. We have a common goal. We want to keep our families safe, so we should just work together."

I rolled my eyes. He was certainly persistent. And gutsy, climbing all that way with no experience. I wasn't stupid. I could see the sense in what he was saying, even if I didn't like the thought of it. There was another problem too, he was a fictional character.

"How do you know you can even leave your story world if we have to?" I asked.

Jack shrugged. "Still not completely convinced I'm in a story, but if it's true, then I'll face that problem when I come to it."

I stared at him. "You're going to risk it all? What if it doesn't work and you just climbed that beanstalk for nothing?"

Jack blanched just a little. "Then I guess I'll go home and sell my cow." He was confident, that was for sure.

"Alright Jack," I said, "I guess you're part of the team. As I said, I'm Cassie. Copper is... around here somewhere." I gazed around and spotted Copper prancing in the grass, nose down, following some scent.

"Allies?" Jack said, raising an eyebrow and holding out a hand.

I hesitated, but I shook his hand. "Allies," I agreed.

Copper bounded over to us and barked loudly. "Shh, Copper!" I scolded. "Somebody will hear you!"

Copper just barked again, jumping around frantically. For a moment, I imagined the cloud ground shaking under us each time he landed. But my imagination couldn't be that vivid. The clouds shook again, even harder this time. I stumbled a little and whirled around. Heading towards us from the castle in the distance, a huge man plodded over the grassy ground. His head was the size of my bedroom back home and one of his hands could easily have crushed all three of us in one swoop.

"Is that a..." Jack began to ask.

"Giant?" I filled in, "Sure is!"

"Fee fie fo fum, I smell the blood of an Englishman. Be he alive or be he dead, I'll grind his bones to make my bread!" the giant's voice boomed out towards us.

Jack paled. "Is he talking about you or me?"

I gave a slightly wicked grin. "I'm not English. Or a man."

The giant had crossed what looked like miles in only a few seconds and was rapidly coming closer.

"We should run," I suggested.

Jack nodded and took off, his exhaustion from the climb forgotten. I picked up Copper and chased after him. Unfortunately, while I had forgotten my exhaustion from the climb, my legs had not and my muscles burned with each step. It was no use anyway. With only a few more thundering steps, the giant was leaning over us, his shadow blocking out the sun.

"We're dead," Jack said, gazing up at the giant over his shoulder, "We're so dead."

"No kidding," I muttered, as the giant's hands reached down and hemmed us in.

Jack and I both tried to scramble out of the way, but the hands were too vast to escape. Meaty fingers closed around us and lifted us up to the giant's face, close enough that I could smell his rancid breath.

Copper squirmed against me, but I couldn't let go of him for fear he might fall. The giant's hand was crushing my lower body in a killer grip.

"Some little snacks for my frying pan," the giant said, "What a lucky day!"

I stayed silent as he lumbered back towards his castle. The shaking was possibly worse when up in the giant's sweaty hand. Each step sent shudders through the giant's whole body, shaking us like we were some kind of rag-dolls.

Once we had reached the castle, which just looked more like a large stone house when we got closer, the giant strode inside. Dumping us into a huge glass jar on the table, he plodded off into the next room. I gazed around. Though the glass slightly warped my view, I could tell we were in a dining room.

"How do we get out?" Jack asked, rubbing his legs which must have felt as crushed as mine did.

"I doubt we could," I told him, "The rim is too high to jump to and the glass is too smooth to climb."

"So... what do we do?" Jack asked.

"Wait for a better opportunity, I guess," I said.

After banging about for a while, in what I assumed was the kitchen, the giant came back clutching a frying pan. Picking up the jar, he tromped back into the kitchen and placed us on the bench.

Copper's claws scratched the glass as the puppy tried to dig us out. It would have been comical if we were not in imminent danger.

The giant placed the frying pan onto the stove and spun the dial to a high heat. Grasping the jar, he tilted it upside-down over the pan and we tumbled out onto the scratched surface of the frying pan.

"Ow," Jack muttered, rubbing his elbow.

My own knees were throbbing where I had landed on them, but now was not the time to worry about that. The pan was warm. It would just keep getting hotter and hotter until we burned up. We were being cooked alive.

"Bert!" came a booming female voice. Another giant, by the sound of it.

"What?" the giant – Bert – yelled back.

"What are you doing in there?" the female giant asked.

"Cooking us some snacks!" Bert shouted.

Their voices hurt my ears, but now wasn't time to worry about that, because I had spotted our escape route. In the bottom of the frying pan, just across from where Jack and I sat, there was a little spark of purple light. It grew larger by the second, expanding like a swirling purple cloud. Nudging Jack with my elbow, I nodded to the portal. Jack's eyes widened. I abruptly came to the realization that if Jack really couldn't go through the portal, then he was left here alone, or maybe worse.

No, Cassie, no! I scolded myself. I couldn't let myself care about that. He was just a storybook character. We were allies for now. Allies with an aligned goal, nothing more. I was wasting time worrying about Jack when Chloe and Dad's lives were on the line.

As the giant continued shouting to his wife, I grabbed Copper by the collar and scrambled over to the portal. Jack followed uncertainly.

"Three, two, one," I whispered, noting the fear in Jack's eyes. He grasped my arm determinedly anyway and we fell, together, into the purple abyss.

It was just as before, only this time I could feel Jack's grip on my wrist. The purple swirling void, the images, the flashing pictures of stories. Then nothing.

My nose twitched. What was that smell? Opening my eyes, I saw I was gazing up at a starry night sky. But that smell... Smoke! It was smoke. And where there was smoke, there was fire! I bolted upright and gazed around. We were in a burning building. Flames leapt all around us. Fire!

In spite of the circumstances, my brain came up with it.

Out of the frying pan into the fire.

CHAPTER SIX
Out of the Frying Pan, Into the Fire

"Run!" I called, tightening my grip on Copper and tugging on Jack's arm. Jack looked slightly dazed, but shook himself out of it when he saw the flames. Copper barked at the leaping fire as Jack and I scrambled to get away. Luckily, the danger wasn't as wide spread as I had thought. Ducking under a blazing beam, I skirted around another patch of fire and raced out of a smoking gap in what appeared to be a wall. We must be in a house. Jack followed right behind me, looking as terrified as I felt.

I had never been a huge fan of fire. It was too hot and too dangerous. I remembered a time when Chloe burned herself on our fireplace at home. Yeah, fire was pretty much a no go for me. Yet here I was.

My muscles were burning, but not from the fire. The toll of the long climb, plus our attempt to run from the giant, and the crushing of the giant's hand around my legs was finally taking effect and I felt like I could barely run anymore.

Abruptly, we burst out of the flames and came out onto a hillside. The ground was bare and dusty here. There was nothing to burn. As long as we were past this area, we would be safe. Behind us, flames stretched up high, lighting the night sky with bright orange fire. I looked back as I ran and gasped. Further on past the house, an entire city was ablaze.

"Mommy!"

I stopped.

"What are you doing?" Jack panted.

"I heard someone," I said, whipping my head around towards the direction the sound had come from. At first, I saw nothing. Then a little head moved in the long grass over on the other side of the hill, close to the burning house. A young girl, no more than eight years old, was cowering on in grass. She wasn't safe. The fire was too close. If the field caught fire, the flames would envelop her. Forgetting my fears and my aching legs, I placed Copper on the ground and rushed over to the girl. Without hesitation, or talking to her first, I picked her up and ran back with her. She sobbed and beat against me with her fists, trying to escape, but I held on to her tightly. When I reached the place where I had left Jack and Copper, I let the girl down.

"Hey," I said softly, giving the little girl a smile. "It's okay. You're safer here. We aren't going to hurt you."

The girl gazed at me. In the moonlight, I could see tears glistening on her cheeks. "My Mommy! I want Mommy!"

"Where is she?" I asked with a sense of foreboding.

"In-in the house," the girl sobbed, "She told me to run. She- she went to get my brother!"

My eyes widened as I gazed back towards the house we had come from. There were people in there? Could I leave them to possibly die?

Something inside me told me no. If there was any way the girl's mother and brother were alive, I had to find them.

"Jack," I said, "take the girl and Copper and go further up the hill. Keep them safe."

Jack's eyes widened as he glanced from me to the fire and back again. "Cassie, you can't be seriously thinking to-"

"I can't let this little girl grow up without her mum!" I interrupted him. "I can't let this woman die."

"So many people will be dying," Jack hissed, gesturing to the fire. "Look how huge this is!"

"Maybe," I said, trying not to think about people dying, "but if I can't save them all, I can at least try and save a few. Don't argue." I looked down at Copper and told him. "Go with Jack."

Copper whined, but I shook my head and pointed at Jack. Turning, I raced back towards the blazing house. All I could think of was that little girl growing up without her family. My own experience flashed in my mind. I had lost my mother. This little girl was just like me in that, but at least I had my mother during most of my childhood. I couldn't let her grow up without a mother.

As I approached the house flames licked at my heels, but I ducked and dodged around them and skidded into the house. Most of the main room was already being devoured by the fire, so I ducked low and crashed right through to the back. Waving to try and clear some smoke away, I peered through the smoke to see a woman standing there. She looked terrified. In her arms was a baby, wrapped up tightly in a blanket. An older boy, maybe six or seven years old, was cowering next to her. Their gazes were fixed on the approaching flames. The mother looked around frantically, as if searching for a way out. The boy looked frozen in fear.

"Hey!" I yelled to get their attention.

The woman and the boy turned to look at me.

"Get down! Get down under the smoke!" I shouted, dropping to the floor myself. "We have to get out of here!"

"There is no way out!" the boy said in a dull voice.

I met his dark blue gaze, so full of resignation that it shocked me, and shook my head. "There's always a way." But as I turned back the way I had come, I saw that the flames had spread, preventing us from leaving that way.

"How?" the woman asked frantically, echoing my thoughts.

I whipped my head around. My throat was sore from breathing in the smoke and I knew we had to get out soon. The room we were in was relatively unaffected by flames, but there was no back door. We were trapped by the flames blazing in the doorway and invading the room. My gaze roamed over the walls, searching for an escape route. Suddenly, through the haze, I caught sight of an opening. It was small and high up, probably just ventilation for airing out the room, but it was not blocked and no flames were near it yet. An exit.

"Up there!" I said, pointing. "That's our way out."

The woman looked desperate and unconvinced. "How will we get up there?"

But the boy's look of defeat and acceptance had been replaced by one of hope. "We can climb Mother. I will help you."

I gave him a smile, impressed by his bravery and willingness to help his mother. Gazing around, I spotted a chair in the corner. I dragged the chair over to the wall. Standing on it, I could reach the grill. After a couple attempts, I managed to shove the grill hatch open. It swung outwards, clearing the way.

"I'll go first," I said. "You can pass me the baby once I'm outside." The woman nodded uncertainly.

I clambered up onto the sill, then squeezed through the gap and dropped onto uneven ground below. Glancing around, I located a large empty barrel that looked like it might've once been used for storage. Rolling it over to the grill opening, I climbed on top so I could reach the gap. The mother reached through and passed the baby to me. I rocked it gently. The child continued sleeping, unaware of the danger he was in. The boy escaped next, slipping easily through the window and landing on the ground. His mother followed, surprisingly agile for a woman of her age. I handed her the baby. We were still in no way safe.

I coughed, trying to clear the smoke from my lungs. "Come on," I called to the woman and her son, "This way."

The three of us skirted around the fire, then headed for where I'd left Jack, Copper and the little girl. Although we were not one hundred percent safe, it was a lot safer than we had been in that tiny room. I noticed the woman glancing back occasionally at the blazing house, which had now collapsed.

"I'm sure you can rebuild," I tried to comfort her.

She just sighed. We continued walking in silence.

"Thank you for saving us."

I nearly jumped. Glancing down, I saw that the boy had left his mother's side and was walking beside me. He slipped his little hand into mine and gazed up at me .

"My name is Felix," the boy said. "You were very brave to come and save us. My mother will be very happy too. She is just worried about my father."

"Where is he?" I asked.

Felix bit his lip. "He went into the big city today. That is where the fires started. Mother is worried that he might be hurt."

Or dead, I added silently, glancing back at the woman. She walked briskly, her eyes on her baby, who'd apparently woken up and started whining.

"What is the big city?" I wondered, thinking about what story we might be in.

Felix gave me a funny look. "You are not from around here, are you? You have weird clothes. Rome, of course."

I nearly froze, but managed to hide my shock. Of course my clothes would be weird in Rome. If we were in Rome, then this may be the Great Fire of Rome. I remembered learning about it in school ages ago. I tried to remember if there had been a specific book or story about it, but my mind blanked. There had to be one, though, because I was in it now. Maybe it was a historical fiction novel. Speaking of Rome, how was I able to understand everyone? Were they all speaking English? Or was I somehow speaking Latin or whatever they spoke in Ancient Rome? Maybe because the book was written in English, it translated for me? Felix's voice snapped me out of my thoughts.

"Claudia!" he called out.

I glanced up to see Copper pelting over the rise, with the little soot-stained girl racing after him.

"Felix! Mother!" Claudia cried out.

"My Claudia!" the woman said. She opened her arms and Claudia rushed into them. The woman held her daughter close. The baby in her arms let out a cry and Claudia broke away from the hug.

"Are you alright?" Felix asked, his eyes wide as he looked at his older sister. "We saw you run into the flames!"

"I made it out," Claudia said. "Jack and Cassie found me and then Cassie went back in to find you and help you."

For the first time since we'd escaped, the mother looked up and met my gaze, her eyes full of sincerity. "Thank you so much. We are very grateful" she said. "My name is Diana. These are my children Claudia, Felix, and Leo."

"Jack," Jack said, reaching out to shake Diana's hand.

"I'm Cassidy," I said, "but you can call me Cassie. This is Copper, my dog." I reached down to stroke him.

Felix's eyes were huge. "I've never seen a dog like that before. Can I touch him?" he asked eagerly. I nodded and Felix cautiously reached out to stroke Copper's silky fur.

"We cannot stay here," Diana said, "Especially if the rain comes. But I'm not sure where we can go."

"The barn Mother!" Claudia piped up. "The barn is far from the fires! That is where Jack took me to stay safe! We can stay in there!" Diana nodded. Jack led the way back to the barn.

It was dawn now. The sun rose over the hills behind us. The fire was still raging, but hadn't come close enough for us to have to move yet.

Claudia, Felix, and Leo were all asleep, worn out by the excitement and terror of the night before.

"Felix mentioned that his father was in the city when the fire started," I said, looking at Diana.

She nodded, her gaze growing distant, "He was. Adrianus was going into the marketplace to sell some of our harvest. Then the fire started. That was four days ago."

"Do you think he's...?" Jack left the question unfinished, but Diana knew what he meant.

"I don't know," she said, tears appearing in her eyes, "I hope that he is safe and alive, but I cannot know for sure. I pray he is alright. I did not think the fire would spread as far as our farm, but it did. It took us by surprise."

"But you're alive," I said, finding myself warming towards her, "and safe for now. So if Adrianus does return, you're here to greet him."

Diana turned to look at me and gave a small smile. "It is thanks to you that I am alive. I had a strange sinking feeling when we were trapped that I was destined to die in that fire. Thank you for saving us, Cassie."

Uncomfortable, I confided, "I- I lost my own mother a couple of years ago now. I couldn't let that happen to Claudia as well. She's so young."

Jack was gazing at me curiously. Maybe he was surprised that I had mentioned my mother's death.

"I'm sorry to hear that," Diana said, kindness and sympathy lacing her tone. "I'm sure she was an amazing woman, to have brought up such a brave girl."

My eyes prickled with tears as I thought about Emma Undering, with her confident grin and positive attitude. I gave a wistful smile. "She was."

As the sun rose, Diana fell asleep on the hay next to her children. I wasn't sure where Jack had gone. I left the young family there with a drowsy Copper as a guardian and headed up to the loft, where sunlight spilled in through a gap in the roof. I gazed out towards Rome and saw the fire blazing. The whole horizon seemed engulfed in flames. I thought about all the people in the city. How many innocent Romans had died over the past few days? I was feeling unsettled.

"What is wrong with me?" I muttered. "I'm not supposed to care! Keep it together Cassie. Copper, Dad, and Chloe, that's it. I can't start caring about anyone else, not even Claudia and Felix." The icy wall I had built around my heart two years ago when my mother died was showing signs of weakness. I didn't want to care. It got too complicated. The more you cared the more you had to lose.

Spotting something moving at the edge of my vision, I whirled around. It was just Jack, hauling himself up into the loft.

"Hey," he said, coming over to me.

"Hey," I replied. For a moment there was silence as we gazed across the acres of field to where the city burned.

Then Jack spoke awkwardly. "For what it's worth, I'm sorry about your mother."

I just stared blankly ahead. "It's not your fault. That's what I don't get. People saying sorry for something that they could never have prevented."

"Well, I guess it is a lousy way to express sympathy," Jack admitted. "I mean that I feel sorry for your loss."

I shrugged. "I don't need your pity."

"I lost my dad," Jack said abruptly. "He was killed by street robbers. There were four of them and one of him. He fought bravely, but they were too strong and they overpowered him. They killed him. Right in front of me. I was too small and weak to stop them. They took our donkey and wagon and everything in it, then hightailed it to the town. I had to walk home to my mother alone. I was only eight years old."

Shocked, I glanced at him and saw a silent tear making its way down his cheek. "That's... terrible."

Jack shrugged, his own gaze fixed on the distant horizon. "When I got home, I vowed I would take care of my mother and never let anything happen to her. And I have, for the past seven years. That's why I'm here. If I just get enough money somehow, I can look after her and make sure she never goes hungry, and will always be safe."

I nodded. "I guess we have more in common than we thought."

He flashed me a sort of sorrowful smile. "I guess we do."

I opened my eyes to find myself lying in the hay, gazing up at a brilliant blue sky. Shifting a little, I glanced at where the fire raged. It was still blazing, smoke wafting into the air, but it seemed a little tamer than usual. Thinking back, I recalled that the Great Fire of Rome had only lasted six days, so we must be nearing the end. Hearing squealing, I crawled over to the edge of the loft and clambered down. It was not extremely high, but I still had that moment at the top where I gazed down and nearly froze up. I know, I know. I'm a climber but I'm afraid of heights. Crazy.

When I reached the floor, two little pairs of hands grabbed at me.

"Cassie! Come play hide and seek with us!" Claudia said.

"Please!" Felix added.

I laughed and I just couldn't say no. "Alright."

It had been years since I had played hide and seek. It was surprisingly fun. Maybe taking my mind off the whole situation for a while was a good thing. After a few rounds, the kids got tired of it and wandered over to their mother to rest. Jack and I climbed back up into the loft.

"Have you seen the purple cloud thing anywhere?" Jack asked me.

I shook my head. "Nah. But... Jack, we can't just leave them here. Not until Diana gets news about Adrianus. We don't know what kind of people are out there that might try to take the food, or hurt the kids. There are desperate people escaping the fire. We can't just disappear on them like that."

Jack glanced back over at where Claudia and Felix were sitting, playing some kind of clapping game. He nodded. "You're right. We can't."

I sighed and gazed out towards the horizon again, where the flames were still ravaging through the city. There would be many mourning families today. There might even be families where nobody was left to mourn.

"You couldn't have done anything about it. No way you could have saved all of them," Jack said.

Startled, I glanced over at him. "How did you-"

"I've been thinking about it too," Jack said, "but you're only one person, Cassie. So am I. Even with two of us, we'd never be able to save the whole of Rome."

I sighed. Abruptly, a flash of light caught my eye. I turned and there, in the roof of the barn, was a swirling portal. My eyes narrowed. The timing of it struck me as a little weird, as well as the placement. Surely it must have been Glorathy's doing. What was Glorathy's plan here? Was there a more mysterious reason for the appearance of the portals and the ease with which everything seemed to work out okay in each story?

I didn't have time to ponder it because there was a squeal of joy from Claudia.

"Father!"

I peered over the edge of the loft and saw Claudia racing towards the barn entrance with Felix on her heels. A tall man with black hair entered the barn, leading a horse.

"Claudia! Felix!" Adrianus cried, laughing as his children jumped at him.

Diana slowly made her way over. As she did, she glanced over her shoulder and met my gaze. Almost as if she knew what I was thinking, she gave me a tiny nod and a small smile. I slipped back down the ladder and fetched Copper, as the reunion went on behind me. Clambering back up to Jack, I offered him my arm.

"To infinity and beyond?" I suggested.

Jack gave me a quizzical look. "What? What does that-"

I cut him off by leaping up into the portal and dragging him in behind me.

CHAPTER SEVEN
Stowaways

After the purple abyss, the flashing images, and the falling, I felt myself smack against hard ground. Opening my eyes, I blinked away the fogginess and found myself staring up at a blue sky. Why was the weather always so nice in story worlds? I mean, aside from the smoke in the last one, but even then, the sky had been mostly clear.

Sitting up, I assessed our situation. We were lying on a grassy hill in the sunshine. Below us, on our left sparkled a vast stretch of water. The ocean. We were by a beach. Copper had wriggled his way out of my grasp once we had landed and was over by a bush that was loaded with red berries, sniffing the ground nearby. A memory flashed back to me. My mother's voice. *These are lingonberries, Cassie. You can eat them if you ever need to when you're stuck in the wild.*

A pang of sadness struck me at the thought of my mother.

Hearing a groan, I glanced at Jack. I realized that he didn't have as much experience with portal-hopping as I did and had not braced for a fall. He was sitting up and rubbing the back of his tousled head where he must have hit it.

"Where are we?" he asked, glancing at me.

I shrugged. "Some hillside? I can't guess the story from this landscape. Are you okay?" I noticed he was still rubbing his head a little dazedly.

Jack nodded. "Yeah. I think I just hit my head pretty hard when we landed."

"Are you hungry?" I asked, shuffling over to the lingonberry bush and plucking some of the juicy red berries off.

Jack stared at me as I popped one into my mouth. "What if those are poisonous?" he asked.

I laughed. "Trust me, if I wasn't sure, I would never eat them. They're lingonberries. Just as edible as blackberries are."

Jack took the berries I offered him. "How do you know this stuff?"

"My mum," I said. I could hear the sorrow tainting my own tone.

"Oh."

We sat in silence and ate our berries. I trawled through my thoughts. I thought about what Jack had said when we in the barn loft, how I couldn't blame myself for not trying to rescue more people from the fire. I knew I shouldn't. Shaking my head, I pulled my locket out from under my shirt and opened it, my gaze lingering on Dad and Chloe's faces. I couldn't let myself care about anyone else. Not when my family's lives were on the line. Who knew what Glorathy Dodge was doing to them? I had to find them! But how? What strange game was going on here?

"Cassie?" Jack waved a hand in front of my face.

I snapped to attention and turned to look at him. "What?"

"Nothing," Jack said, grinning. "You just zoned out for a second there. I figured we should get going."

I almost grinned back, but stopped myself, not wanting build a friendship with my 'ally.' That would make it too complicated. Hurriedly, I stood up and whistled to Copper.

"We should go find water," I told Jack. "Before we, you know, die of dehydration."

His eyes narrowed, as if he detected my sudden change in mood, but he just shrugged and nodded. "Alright," he said. "Let's head down to the shore and see if we can find a river running into the sea."

I agreed and we started off down the hill. It helped that there appeared to be a path that many people usually took to make their way up. The trees and bushes had been cleared to create a path of sorts. Copper took the lead, bounding off down the hill, barking whenever he spotted a rabbit. Which was every few minutes.

"What are we supposed to do here? There must be people in this story, right?" I asked after a few minutes of silence. "Or... other things?"

Jack glanced at me. "What 'other things' do you mean?"

"Like dragons and unicorns and mermaids and stuff," I elaborated. "You know, mythical fantasy creatures."

Jack squinted. "What are dragons and uni-cons and mermads? Are they animals like cows and donkeys?"

I laughed and spent a couple minutes trying to explain dragons in a way that Jack would understand. Eventually, I gave up.

"Never mind," I said, shaking my head, "You'd know one if you saw one."

"Okay," Jack said with laughter in his voice.

Copper suddenly let out a fierce growl and barked loudly. I whipped my head around to look at him. He'd spotted another dog. A little black and white spotted dog, ragged and dirty with its tail well between its legs, was cowering as Copper barked at it.

"Hey, Copper!" I shouted, "Heel!" Copper snarled once more at the dog, then trotted back over to me.

"What's up with you?" I said, crouching down to look my dog in the eye, "You're not usually so fierce." Copper sniffed the air and barked again. As I prepared to reprimand him, the scent came to my nose too. Salt. We were nearing the ocean. That was what had Copper so excited.

"Do you think that little dog came from over there?" Jack asked.

I straightened and followed where he was pointing to see a little dock town in the shelter of a cliff. Several large ships were resting there, alongside a smattering of smaller ones. Houses stretched from the base of the cliff to where the sand began.

"Oh!" I exclaimed. "I can't believe we didn't see that before."

Copper turned to look at me, then back over at the sparkling sea, his tail wagging to and fro like the broken needle on a compass. He gave a bark that was more like a yip.

"Do we... head over there?" Jack asked.

I paused, pondering. What if the people in the town weren't friendly? What if they tried to hurt us in some way? We didn't know what story this was. My mind flicked through all the stories I had read, trying to find one where there was a village by the sea. Too many possibilities.

"Hello? Cassie?" Jack waved a hand in front of my face.

I swerved to look at him. "Um... I'm not sure. What if-"

Before I had a chance to finish sharing my worries, Copper gave a joyful bark and took off down the path towards the town.

Jack laughed. "I guess that's our answer."

I couldn't help smiling. We both raced after Copper.

The town was a little spooky up close. Even though it was broad daylight, there were only a few people around in what appeared to be the town center. A well sat in the center of the town square, but I didn't trust it enough to drink from it. We'd find a natural source later. Occasionally, someone would come out of one of the houses, but they would keep their head down and hurry on. After this happened a few times, I glanced over at Jack. He looked just as weirded out by it as I felt.

Once we reached the docks, it was livelier. People had stalls set up by the shore and were selling wares. Fish, fish hooks, strings, ocean treasures. I kept Copper close, not wanting to lose him in the crowd. As we strode through the marketplace, I noticed that one of the large ships had its sails raised, ready to sail.

"We have to get on that boat," I whispered. I wasn't sure where the urge came from, but I was sure of it. I grabbed Jack's arm, making him jump. "We have to get on that boat," I repeated, louder this time.

Jack gave me a strange look. "Are you sure? I'm not sure I would trust these people."

"They don't have to know," I hissed, staring at him urgently. "I just... I can feel it. The portal will be something to do with that ship."

Jack raised an eyebrow but I glared at him, defiant. "Fine." He sighed. "How do we get on the boat?"

I grinned. "We stowaway."

It turned out coming up with the idea of stowing away was much easier than actually doing it. It took about four tries to get into the ship's cargo hold unnoticed. The gruesome looking woman with an eye-patch, at the front of the dock where the boat was, had an eagle eye. When she looked away to yell at two men who were loading a barrel together, Jack and I slipped on board. I carried Copper so he wouldn't fall into the sloshing water next to the dock.

The ship, called the Flying Seagull, wasn't in top notch condition. It seemed as if it had been patched up with boards many times. The crew matched their ship, dirty and scarred, with some having eye-patches or peg-legs. I didn't want to think about what they might do if they caught us.

Jack found a quiet corner in the hold, between two large crates where we could hide away without anyone seeing us. Tucked into the corner, I shuddered each time the boat rocked with another wave, as it started on its journey. I didn't trust it one bit, nor did I trust the people on it. But we were here now and it was not like getting off was an option.

Jack tentatively reached out and put his hand on my arm. He was nervous too, I could tell from his sweaty hand and quickening pulse. Normally, I'd want to shake free of his hand. I didn't need the hassle of friendship. But we were allies. And allies helped each other, right?

Every time the ship rocked, I worried it might be torn apart. Copper looked like he wanted to bark and growl, but I kept a hand on his collar and he understood the need to be quiet. Faint shouts came from above as the crew rushed about on deck.

"Where do you think this ship is going?" Jack whispered, peering out from behind the crate. I copied him. Nobody was around.

"I don't know," I said. "I don't really trust these people."

Copper gave me a look, as if he was saying 'when do you trust anyone?'. I narrowed my eyes at him.

"But you seemed pretty determined to get on this boat," Jack said. "You must have had some indication of where it's going."

"I... no," I said, cringing inwardly. I didn't want to explain my feeling that we had to get on this boat. I didn't really understand it myself. It would be weird and awkward on too many levels. From the look Jack was giving me, he already thought I was crazy.

"Hopefully the trip's not too long then," Jack said a little perturbed, "because we still don't have any water."

"Or food," I pointed out, leaning back to rest my head on the wall and gazing upwards. The roof of the cargo hold was a meter above my head. Small spaces didn't bother me, so I wasn't worried. Until something furry scurried over my foot. A scream nearly broke free of my mouth as I snapped my gaze down and it fastened on a rat the size of a soccer ball. It was massive. I immediately put a restraining hand on Copper. The rat blinked at me in the half dark, then scrambled away. Copper whined and looked after it longingly, as if he wanted to chase it, but he stayed put.

"I hope that, wherever we're going, it isn't too far away," I whispered.

Jack nodded. "And I hope it's not as stuffy and rancid as this place."

I agreed, "Yeah. And I hope the portal's there."

We sat in silence for a few seconds, then Jack spoke. "You said you want your family back," he said tentatively, "Your dad?"

"And my sister," I nodded. "They were taken by Glorathy." I explained what had happened. "I can't help feeling like this is all a game to her. It seems like she is sending me through different stories. Did she orchestrate my saving Diana and Leo and Felix, and then feeling bad about being unable to save anyone else? I don't know. But she's definitely messing with me."

"You think she has a bigger plan?" Jack guessed.

I bit my lip. "I'm saying that it's possible that we're just pawns in her little game. We're doing everything she wants us to. But why? It doesn't make any sense."

"Maybe you're overthinking it," Jack suggested, though he glanced away as he said it. I was about to reply when the whole ship gave an almighty shudder and a shriek came from above.

"Run! Abandon ship!"

"Get out of here!"

Pounding footsteps slapped on the deck above us. Jack and I exchanged a glance. The ship shook again. Scooping Copper up, I crawled out of our hiding place and scrambled for the ladder, Jack close behind.

We emerged onto the deck in the midst of a rain of fire. It felt almost like deja vu. Gazing around, I spotted people clambering into lifeboats, shoving at each other to get in first. In the middle of all the chaos, I realized something.

"Pirates!" I exclaimed. When Jack looked at me quizzically, I elaborated, "They're pirates! Thieves, back-stabbers and no-good."

"Great," Jack said, rolling his eyes, "So glad we're on a burning ship full of them."

"Why is the ship burning?" I wondered aloud.

As if in answer to my question, another round of flames fell from above. Wait, from above? I glanced up and choked back a scream. Jack must have seen the look on my face, because he followed suit and froze.

"What is that?" he whispered hoarsely, staring up at the two-headed red beast that was circling above us with vast sweeps of its massive wings.

My gaze was also fixed on the scaly creature as I replied, "That, Jack, is a dragon."

The dragon swooped around and zoomed back towards us, blasting fire onto one of the lifeboats. As we watched, I suddenly realized that one of the huge heads had its yellow eyes fastened on us. The dragon turned towards Jack and I.

"Jack, run!" I said, tugging on his arm.

Jack seemed paralyzed with fear, staring as the dragon bore down on us. I loosened my grip on Jack, prepared to make a break for it on my own, but something inside me caused me to stall. In that moment of hesitation, the dragon's claws fastened around my middle and I was lifted into the air. Copper yelped and squirmed in my arms, but I held tight. The sharp pointed ends of the claws dug into my side, but I was too afraid to care. My breathing quickened as I stared down at the ocean far below me. "Don't drop me," I whispered, the world seeming to spin as the ship became just a speck on a sea of blue, "Please don't drop me."

I hugged Copper closer and glanced over at the dragon's other foot, kind of relieved to see Jack dangling there. I met his wide eyed gaze. Why hadn't I just run and saved me and Copper? Look where it got me.

Somehow, I must have passed out, because when I opened my eyes, I was in a huge cavern, with a rocky ceiling looming high above. I had never been so happy to feel solid ground underneath me. Sitting up, I gazed around. Copper was curled up at my side, his tail swishing gently and making clinking noises every time he shifted the… coins? I was sitting on a massive pile of gold coins. Gazing around, I let out a gasp. Gold, as far as the eye could see. Mounds of it, some piled up as high as the ceiling. We were in a cave full of sparkling gold and jewels. This had to be the dragon's lair. Next to me, Jack was sitting up, uncomfortably perched on the jewels. "I've been pretending to be asleep, but the dragon's gone now," he told me.

As he gazed around, his eyes widened to the size of saucers. "There's no way that dragon needs all this gold, right?" Jack murmured, picking up a handful and letting the coins trickle through his fingers. He stood up. His eyes were shining as he overlooked the towering piles of precious materials.

"Jack," I warned, glancing around warily, "You shouldn't take this stuff. I don't think the dragon will appreciate it."

Jack wasn't listening to me. Greed shone in his eyes as he stuffed his pockets full of gemstones and coins. As he did, I heard a fiery roar from the other end of the cave. It reverberated through the cavern.

"Jack," I said, my eyes widening, "That's our cue to leave!"

Jack looked torn. "My mother would never starve if we had all this gold..." he muttered.

There was a thud and the red, two headed dragon burst around a mountain of gold. It narrowed its eyes at us, wings stretched high and flames flaring from its nostrils.

"Run!" I shouted, darting away with Copper at my heels.

Jack stayed, frozen to the spot, pockets bulging with stolen gold. Again, I felt that pang inside me. I couldn't leave Jack to become dragon fodder. Growling in frustration, I raced back, gripped Jack's arm firmly and dashed away again, yanking him along with me.

Jack came to life again as we ran, pelting away from the sound of thudding footsteps and clinking coins behind us. We were too slow. The bulk of heavy jewels in Jack's pockets were constricting his movements and weighing him down.

"Jack, get rid of the money!" I yelled.

"What?" Jack shouted back. "No! My mother needs this gold!"

"She also needs you to be alive!" I yelled back. "Drop the jewels, Jack!"

Reluctantly, Jack started yanking handfuls of coins and and jewels out of his various pockets and dropping them on the ground. He lingered over a huge ruby. That dragon would never stop chasing us if he kept it.

"Drop it!" I screamed, while searching frantically for an escape route.

Thundering footsteps neared. Jack tossed the ruby to the side and we gained speed. My gaze flicked from side to side, scanning for an exit. Suddenly I saw it. As always, seemingly on cue, the portal appeared just a little way ahead in the cave wall.

"There!" I nodded to it with my head. We raced up to the portal. It was our freedom. Just before we reached it, Jack stopped. Bending down, he picked up an emerald, seriously nearly as big as my head, from yet another pile of treasure.

"Leave it, Jack!" I shouted over the sound of the dragon's pounding footfalls.

He didn't move. "My mother needs this!"

The dragon came into sight. Its yellow eyes narrowed and it reared back to breath fire. Just as the fire was about to turn us into barbecue, I knocked the gem out of Jack's hands and dragged him with me through the portal.

The last thing I saw as I spun around, was what appeared to be a ladle-wielding chicken chasing a ragged pirate out of a nearby side cave, and I wondered what strange tale we had been in. Then the odd scene was gone as we descended into the now familiar purple wormhole.

CHAPTER EIGHT
Wits and Weapons

"You idiot!" I yelled at Jack as soon as we landed, "You could've gotten us all killed!"

Jack narrowed his eyes. "I needed that money for my mother! We don't have enough food, or clothes, or medicine, or anything! She could die!"

"*We* could've died!" I fired back, "I need to make it to Glorathy to save my family!"

"Why didn't you just leave me to die then?" Jack suggested, his gaze furious, "And go save your family! I can make my own decisions."

Silence. I didn't want to admit the truth. We stared at each other. Jack's hands, which had been balled into fists, slowly unclenched.

"Admit it, you're not as uncaring as you make out, are you?" Jack asked. "We're friends now, and you don't leave friends behind. You don't want to leave me behind."

"No!" I protested. "That's not it. I don't care! We're allies though as long as it suits." Even to me, my tone was unconvincing.

Jack cocked his head on the side. "Why do you insist on only caring about a certain few people? What about friends, Cassie?"

"Friends aren't worth it. You only end up getting hurt," I said in a distant voice. "When you love someone all it does is increase the chance of getting hurt. It's better to just not care. If I hide away in the shadows, nobody notices me, nobody speaks to me, nobody cares about me, and I don't care about anybody."

Jack frowned, his piercing gaze fixed on me. "If you have no impact on the world around you, what's the point of even being alive?"

I couldn't think of anything to say to that. Thankfully, I didn't have to, because Copper chose that moment to let out a loud bark and dart off towards a squirrel who was sitting at the bottom of a nearby tree. I took the chance to look around. The squirrel scampered away, leaving a disappointed Copper at the bottom of the trunk. We had landed in a forest. It seemed like mostly oak trees, with acorns littering the ground and green leaves blotting out the sky.

"I wonder what story this is?" I murmured, almost to myself.

Jack, who had evidently given up on the conversation, shrugged. "You'd know better than me."

"I guess we should get moving," I said, looking anywhere but at his face. The tension and awkwardness between us had only faded a little.

"Yeah, to find the portal," Jack agreed.

I whistled for Copper and the three of us set out, wandering through the woods. Occasionally, a fallen log or a dense bush or a muddy patch of ground would block our path and we'd make a detour.

Eventually, I spotted something through the trees. As we drew closer, I realized it was a tiny cottage with white stone walls and a wooden roof. We emerged into the clearing that contained the house and I gasped. I recognized this place.

"What?" Jack asked, wrinkling his nose as he untangled a thick strand of cobweb from his messy brown hair. I assumed we both looked a mess from the combination of ash, mud, and whatever else we'd picked up on our travels.

"This house," I said, "I know it." The picture was branded in my mind. It was my favourite fairy tale, the one I used to beg my mother to read to me over and over again. "We're in Snow White," I said. My eyes were wide as I gazed around, suddenly feeling like a little kid again. When I was younger, I had always wanted to be Snow White.

"Am I supposed to know what that means?" Jack asked a little testily.

"Nah," I replied, a huge grin appearing on my face, "but it's really cool for me." Just as soon as it appeared, my grin faded. My mother would have loved to have been here with me.

"What happens in Snow White?" Jack asked.

"Basically, there's this girl who's really pretty," I began, "Her mum dies and her dad marries this beautiful lady, but his new wife is really vain. This stepmother, she has this magic mirror that she always asks, *Who is the most fair in the land?* Usually the mirror says it's her, but one day it says, *Snow White*. The stepmother is mad and orders a huntsman to kill her stepdaughter, Snow White. The huntsman takes Snow White into the woods but he can't bring himself to kill her, so he just leaves her there. Snow White wanders alone for a while until she comes to a house. This house," I pointed at the little cottage, "where seven dwarves live and-" I broke off, staring across the clearing as a wagon pulled up. An old woman with a hooded cloak and a basket of what looked like ribbons was driving it.

Stopping at the door, the woman leapt nimbly off her wagon and hurried up to the door.

Quietly, I approached, pressing against the side of the cottage. As Jack followed me, I gave Copper a warning look that said stay. He plonked down on the ground, dejected. Creeping up to the edge of the house, I cautiously peeked around. The old woman was laughing creakily. A young girl had just fallen at her feet. Snow White. The old hag cackled as she strode back to her wagon, clambered on, and rode away into the woods. I raced up to Snow White.

"What happened?" Jack asked, his face a mask of confusion.

"That woman was her stepmother," I said, bending down over Snow White.

She really was beautiful. Her black hair was silky and shiny, her skin was perfectly smooth, and her face was like a porcelain doll.

"Really? You said the stepmother was beautiful," Jack said.

"She's magic, Jack," I said. "She used a disguising spell. She tricked Snow White into..." I paused. What was it? A lace! That was it. "A magic lace on her bodice thing! She tricked Snow into letting her put it on too tight so that she can't breathe."

Jack crouched down and brushed Snow's hair away, revealing the silky ribbon.

"Wait!" I said as Jack reached around to untie the lace.

"What? She's going to die, Cassie!" Jack said.

I bit my lip. "But... the dwarves are supposed to come back and save her." Was it possible to spoil this well loved children's story?

"She could die!" Jack repeated, staring at me. And I realised we had already done that with Jack's story. I groaned, clenching and unclenching my fists. Snow would be fine, I told myself. I didn't need to help.

But I couldn't just leave her.

"Okay," I muttered. I fell to my knees next to Jack and rolled Snow onto her side so that Jack could undo the ribbon off the bodice.

My hand unconsciously snaked its way up to grab the locket under my shirt. I had to focus, and my focus was saving my family. The ones I really loved.

Meanwhile, Jack was helping Snow White sit up. "What happened?" she asked. The stories had gotten something right. Her voice sounded musical; soft and sweet.

"Your stepmother was disguised as that old crone," Jack explained. "She tried to suffocate you with this." He held the ribbon up to show her.

Snow White's striking blue eyes widened. "Oh my!" she exclaimed, her hand fluttering to her brow. It was all I could do not to roll my eyes. As nostalgic as this was for me, I didn't remember Snow White being so... posh and princess-like. I guess when my mother was reading the book to me I always pictured Snow White a little... tougher.

"You shouldn't open up the door to that woman again," Jack advised. I shot him a look. I wasn't sure how much of the story we were supposed to tell Snow. Would we ruin Snow White forever? What if we already had? Jack clearly didn't have the same reservations. "Your stepmother has already tried to kill you twice," he said. "You need to defend yourself from her."

Snow White blinked slowly. "Defend myself?" She glanced back and forth between Jack and I. I realized how crazy we must seem. I was wearing blue jeans and a purple t-shirt, not exactly something that people in Snow White's story would wear. Even Jack in his ragged clothes stuck out next to Snow White's spotless dress and apron. Both of us were covered in ash, mud, and some green substance from the beanstalk that stained our clothing. To Snow White, we probably seemed a little nuts.

"I do thank you ever so much, for releasing me from my stepmother's evil trick," Snow White said, her voice airy and delicate. I ground my teeth together in frustration. Was this what talking to her would always be like? Lots of blinking eyelashes and softly spoken words?

"You're welcome," I muttered.

"What are your names?" Snow asked. "I am Snow White."

"I'm Cassie," I said. "This is Jack, and-" I broke off, realizing Copper wasn't with us. Letting out a sharp whistle, I heard an excited yip and Copper tore around the corner of the cottage, racing up to me, his tail wagging like crazy. "This is Copper," I finished, commanding the enthusiastic puppy to sit.

Snow's wide eyes rounded even more and she broke into a perfect movie-star worthy grin. "Oh! What a lovely dog! It's so small and soft!" Bending down, she stroked Copper's silky fur.

The ground began to shake, just a little. Snow continued to play with Copper's fur and Jack continued laughing at the dog's antics, but Copper glanced at me, almost as if to check that I had felt it too. I frowned.

A moment later it happened again. This time, the trees shuddering too. The house next to us creaked slightly.

"Guys-" I began.

Copper let out a loud bark and began to growl.

"What?" Jack asked, glancing at me.

"Can you feel that... shaking?" I asked.

The earth shook again, as if answering me. Jack had to steady Snow as she stood up.

"What is happening?" she exclaimed, her mouth shaped into a perfect O.

I rolled my eyes. "Look Snow, I appreciated the princess-like manner in the book, but not so much in real life. Get some wits and maybe a weapon. Whatever it is that's making that sound, it's probably not anything friendly."

I had a weird feeling in my stomach, like when I had known we had to board the ship. Inexplicably, I knew that something from another story world was in this one. Something troublesome and dangerous. Something evil.

"Oh!" Snow's eyes widened at my harsh words, and she looked majorly confused, but I didn't have time to care. I didn't want to care either.

"We should head for the village," I said. "There will be weapons there. Snow, what direction is the town?"

Snow turned to glance at the forest. "That way... I think," she pointed.

"Great, let's go," I said.

"Woah, Cassie," Jack said, grabbing my arm. "You can't just charge in there. It'll be dangerous!"

"I just have a feeling about this! I don't think our portal exit will appear if we don't find and stop whatever it is making that shaking," I said.

Jack narrowed his eyes, then shrugged. "I guess you were right last time. OK let's go."

Snow led us to the village, where people ran around screaming about terrible beasts coming to attack them. For the first time, I noticed what poorly described story people looked like. They were sketchy looking, a bit like a rushed 3D drawing that didn't quite turn out right. Their whole village was the same.

As we approached, nobody seemed to notice us. They were all too busy panicking. After witnessing one man drop his sword on the ground in a frantic hurry to flee, Jack picked it up, weighing the slightly insubstantial looking blade. Shrugging, he tucked it into his belt.

"Do you know how to use that?" I asked.

He shrugged again. "I'm sure it's simpler than it looks."

I raised an eyebrow. Hiding a grin, I gazed around, looking for something I could use. My gaze fastened on a bow, balanced atop a quiver of arrows, on the veranda of a nearby house. I raced over and picked it up. It looked as insubstantial as anything else in the town, but it felt the same as other bows I had used before. I had an uneasy feeling this was too easy. How come we had been able to find weapons so quickly?

I didn't have time to ponder it because at that moment, with a particularly massive quake, the beast that was making the noise came into view. It approached from the direction of the forest, crushing trees under its feet.

"What is that thing?" Jack shouted over the noise of people screaming.

I just shook my head, staring at the vast creature. It reminded me a little of Danger, only much, much larger. It was the size of a house, with dark fur and tiny purple eyes. It's shape was more of a cube than Danger's was, with thick, muscly arms that reached to the ground, claws dragging in the dirt. As it drew nearer, I could make out a small mouth with tiny sharp teeth. It looked slightly comical on the massive beast.

"What do we do?" Jack asked, looking at me. "These aren't going to be much use against that!" He held up his sword.

Why was it up to me to think of a plan? Didn't Jack have a brain too? Couldn't he have an idea for once?

"Uh…" I stuttered, my eyes flicking around as I searched frantically for an answer. My mind was blank of ideas. All I could think about was Dad and Chloe and how much I wanted to see them. They needed me right now. But at the same time, I couldn't let everybody in this village die. And it seemed that the path to them, led through all these 'distractions'.

Here I go again, I thought. Hopefully this time, saving the people would get me another step closer to saving my family.

"I have a plan," Snow White said.

Both Jack and I stared at her. I raised an eyebrow. Even Copper looked skeptical. But there was a new light of determination in Snow's eyes as she glanced at the monster that was fast approaching, each of its footfalls causing a small earthquake.

"We need to rally my people," Snow said, gazing around, "They will help us fight."

Glancing around at the fleeing citizens, I frowned. They didn't look like they were up to a fight. They looked terrified. But Jack and I followed Snow White anyway as she hitched up her skirt and raced towards the center of town.

"My people!" she shouted, gathering everyone's attention, "I am your princess, Snow White! We must work together to defeat this evil beast who is trying to destroy our town!"

Even though some of the people looked a little suspicious, after shouting this out a few times, the words of the beautiful, determined young girl seemed to be enough, whether they believed she was Snow White or not. People stopped running and looked around to gather weapons. They gathered together and set off marching in the direction of the approaching giant monster. Even the women joined in, although the children were made to stay back in the more sturdy houses. More and more people joined in as we strode towards the beast. Once we reached the other end of town, we were face to face with the creature.

"Leave our town alone!" Snow cried out valiantly.

Others joined in. I frowned. I was pretty sure that the monster wouldn't just back off by being yelled at. As I gazed up into its round purple eyes, I thought I spotted a spark of intelligence. There was also a glint of malice.

Gasping, I nocked an arrow in my bow, but before I could shoot, the monster reached out, plucked up a handful of villagers, and shoved them into its mouth. I fired, my arrow bouncing off the beast's arm. It must have pretty thick skin.

I expected chaos to ensue, people to flee in panic, the monster to rampage. Instead, Snow charged forward, her sword raised, and most of her people followed suit, slashing and stabbing at the parts of the creature they could reach. This just seemed to make it angrier.

I loaded another arrow, trying to push the image of the monster's cruel action out of my head. I shot again, this time the arrow hit the creature's eye. It roared in pain, even though the arrow seemed to bounce off the tough skin of its eyelid. Lashing out, the angry monster knocked a few townspeople to the ground. I tried not to think about it. If I cared too much I would lose my focus. I shouldn't care, they were just fictional characters anyway.

But you do care, a little voice in my head whispered.

I shut it down and aimed another arrow.

Jack suddenly appeared beside me. "Aim for the mouth."

I glanced at him, raising an eyebrow. "What?"

"Aim for its mouth when it roars," Jack repeated. "It's the only weak point as far as I can see."

I narrowed my eyes, checking out the creature. It was true. Other than the eyes, the mouth was the most vulnerable. I might even get its brain. I shifted my aim, waiting for the thing to open its hideous mouth. When it did, I released my arrow. It flew, straight and true, into the monster's mouth, disappearing into the gaping hole. The creature howled in pain and clawed at its mouth, trying to grab the arrow, but the projectile had gone in too far. The monster fell. Some of the townspeople didn't get out of the way quickly enough. I cringed at the thud as the giant creature hit the ground.

But we had done it. We had defeated the monster.

Somehow it didn't it feel like a victory.

"We lost about forty people, Your Majesty," a vague looking 3D man told Snow White.

She nodded. "Thank you. You may go and tend to your family."

The man hurried away.

I flinched. Most of the deaths were my fault. In fact, I had a sneaking suspicion that if I weren't in this story in the first place, none of this would have happened. Somehow the fact that they were fictional characters didn't make any difference. It still felt bad.

Our portal had appeared in the castle a couple of minutes ago, as we were exploring and wondering what to do next. Jack and I had come to say goodbye to Snow White.

"Jack! Cassie!" Snow said, smiling as she turned to look at us.

"We're leaving," I said bluntly.

Snow's smile stayed put. "Oh... well that is a shame. I truly hope you have safe travels. Remember, you are always welcome here."

I couldn't help smiling back. After all, Snow White wasn't too bad. I only wished my mother could have been here with me.

Jack nodded. "Thanks for everything."

Snow nodded back. "I should be thanking you. Are you sure you don't want to stay?"

"We're sure," I said. "Come on Jack."

We headed back to the highest tower room. A swirling purple portal awaited us, sunken into the floor. Copper, who had been sitting at the portal waiting, barked and stood up. I scooped him up and grabbed Jack's hand.

"Ready?" I asked.

Jack nodded, a smirk on his face. "I wonder what story we'll crash this time."

I rolled my eyes and dragged him into the purple abyss.

CHAPTER NINE
Desperate Times

When we landed, I released Copper and jumped up immediately. I had done this enough times to know that I had to be prepared for anything. Sniffing, I knew we had to be near the ocean once more. The distinct smell of salt water hung in the air. Turning around, I could see the ocean, sparkling and blue, stretched out in a wide bay. There was a nasty clump of jagged rocks on the shore near the entrance to the bay. I thought I spotted some floating wood there, but I was too far away to be sure.

Copper let out a bark and bounded away towards the far end of the beach, his paws kicking up sand. I gazed around, scanning my surroundings. Tall cliffs bordered the beach on three sides, while the ocean covered the fourth. A small river flowed into the sea near the other end of the beach, where Copper was headed. I couldn't see anything that clued me in as to what story it was yet. I reminded myself to keep a lookout.

Hearing a groan, I nearly jumped out of my skin, before realizing it was just Jack. A little way up the beach from where I was, he sat up and brushed the sand off his clothes and hair.

"Why can't the landings be just a little gentler?" he muttered, rubbing the back of his head where he must have hit it.

"At least this time we landed on sand," I said, leaning down to scoop up a handful and let it trickle through my fingers.

"I must have hit some really hard sand then," Jack grumbled, glancing down at the stones where he had landed. "Do you know this story yet?" he asked, stumbling a little as he stood up.

I rolled my eyes. "Ah yes, a beach with cliffs around it and an ocean. Could be about a million different books."

Jack frowned. "It was just a question."

"A stupid one," I muttered under my breath.

I knew I was being mean and unnecessarily blunt, but I was having a weird time controlling how I felt about my 'ally'. I didn't want to care about Jack. We were allies, nothing more. I didn't want to care about what happened to him. I couldn't. He was a fictional character for goodness sake, and he had already caused me to be distracted from my mission. My focus had to be on getting my family back, and no one was going to slow me down, need rescuing, or distract me.

"Uh… Cassie?" Jack waved a hand in front of my face.

I snapped back to reality. "What?"

"Where's Copper?" he asked.

I whipped my head around, but the dog was nowhere to be seen. "Copper!" I shouted.

A faint bark came from the end of the beach where I had last seen Copper. I started running, not caring that my shoes would probably be filled with sand by the time I got there. The sort of shuffling, thudding noise behind me told me that Jack was following. We came to the end of the beach and stopped. Copper sat beside the river, looking pleased with himself. Next to him, spanning the width of the river, was a wooden bridge.

Someone had obviously been here before. It should not have been a surprise. Every story had to have at least one main character and this was part of the story, but still.

"It looks a bit rickety, do you think it is safe?" Jack asked.

Something triggered in my memory as I stared at the bridge. I glanced back over my shoulder at the bay. I remembered another story my mother read to me and my older sister when we were younger. Swiss Family Robinson, a story about a family of six getting stranded on an island after their ship wrecked in a storm. I wasn't one hundred percent sure of it, but it seemed it could fit.

"Cassie!" Jack said, jolting me out of my thoughts. I turned to glance at him.

"That's the third time I said your name," Jack said, "What are you thinking about?"

"I think I might know what story we're in," I told him.

"Okay, what is it?" Jack asked.

"Swiss Family Robinson," I said.

Jack shrugged. "Never heard of it."

I gave him a pointed look. "You're a book character, Jack."

Jack frowned. "It's so weird to think about."

I shrugged. "Yeah, I guess it must be."

"Yeah – woah, what is that?" Jack stared at something behind me.

I whirled around to see some kind of shimmery patch hanging in the air a little way down the beach. It was kind of like a rippling patch of water, only it was in the air. Cautiously, I wandered over and reached up to touch it. Jerking back immediately, I stared. It felt sort of rough and yet insubstantial, like a piece of strained fabric that had been stretched too tight and was tearing apart in the middle. The shape of it seemed to be getting gradualy larger and occasionally flashed with purple sparks. I knew one thing for sure.

It wasn't part of the story.

"What do you think it is?" Jack asked from right beside me. I jumped. I hadn't heard him follow me.

"I don't know," I said, examining the rippling patch from all angles.

Jack squinted at it, as if thinking. Carefully, he reached out to touch it, running his fingers over the centre. I peered at it closely. It almost seemed as if his fingers sort of sank into the shimmering patch of air.

A vague shadowy shape flitted past the shiny spot and I gasped.

"Did you see that?" I asked.

Jack nodded. He turned to look at me. "What if it's a sort of tear?"

I blinked at him, my brow crinkling. "What?"

"Like... uh... an unintended opening," Jack explained, "A tear in the fictional world. A worn through spot where the wall between the worlds is wearing thin."

I squinted at the 'tear.' It made sense. "Kind of like a rift.... With all the portals Glorathy's made, the borders of each story may be wearing thin in places, or affected in some way."

"Exactly," Jack agreed. He brushed his fingers over the tear again. "And because she's carrying on making portals, the rifts will get more and more frequent until the fictional worlds are connected in many places, along with being connected to what you call the real world. Like you said, she has made portals there."

My eyes widened at the thought of that. There had already been chaos when the Hungry Caterpillar had gotten lose. What would happen if the Evil Queen escaped? Or giants? Most of the characters from the stories I had been to so far had been too preoccupied in their own stories to notice the portals – even Snow White had never asked questions – but that wouldn't last if the barriers between the stories were destroyed.

"That would be a disaster," I whispered.

Jack nodded. "Another reason why we have to stop Glorathy."

I turned to him, raising an eyebrow. "Aren't you only in this for the money?"

Jack stared at me for a second, then shrugged and turned away. "We should go find the next portal and maybe we can find Glorathy."

Something in his tone told me I shouldn't argue, so I shrugged as well and we headed back up the beach to where Copper was waiting patiently beside the bridge.

As we crossed the bridge carefully and headed through the trees on a trail of sorts, I zoned out, thinking about what I would do after saving Dad and Chloe. If I saved Dad and Chloe. I couldn't bear to think about any other outcome.

Would I just go back to normal life? I had a feeling my life would never be the same again. It was weird to think about going back to school again after I had escaped from a witch, a giant, pirates, a dragon, and more crazy creatures.

And what about Jack?

I frowned. What about Jack? He would just go back to his story with whatever gold or treasure we managed to obtain from Glorathy wouldn't he?. He'd go back to his family, I'd go back to mine. Our temporary alliance would be over. I felt a pang in my heart that felt way too much like sadness for my liking.

I couldn't care about what happened to Jack. And I didn't. I was sure of it.

I stood on the back of Jack's shoe by accident. He had stopped in the middle of the path.

"There's another one," he said.

I followed his hand to where he was pointing and could see that he was right. Another shimmery rift hung in the air. This one was tiny compared to the first, and just as insubstantial looking. Copper growled at it, as if he knew the chaos it could cause.

"This is so weird," I murmured, the surreality of the situation hitting me like a slap in the face. "An evil sorceress, who opened portals between all the fictional worlds, has stolen my dad and sister and threatened to kill them. I have traveled to the worlds of all these stories that my mum used to read me. Now the borders between the worlds are breaking down because of all the portals and I'm supposed to stop it."

"We," Jack corrected.

I glanced at him. The determination in his gaze was impossible to miss. This was obviously about more than just gold for him. When had he grown a conscience?

"Allies, remember?" he said, grinning and raising an eyebrow.

I shrugged. "Yeah."

We continued walking in silence until we came to the bottom of a massive boulder. Many meters taller than me and nearly four times as wide, the rock cast a vast shadow down on us.

I wondered vaguely if this was what writers meant what they talked about being at rock bottom. In the darkness.

Jack crouched down and picked up a rock from the ground at the base of the boulder. It was a pebble in comparison. "Cassie, look at this!" he exclaimed, his eyes widening.

I raised an eyebrow. It was just a rock. But he seemed weirded out, so I headed over to him. He showed me the rock. Part of it was a normal, gray, slightly dusty rock. The other part looked like the time I had mixed my raspberry yogurt with neon purple slime when I was four years old. It was a sort of sparkly purple, that flashed translucent occasionally. Not natural.

"Do you think it's to do with the borders breaking down?" I asked, taking the rock from him.

Jack nodded. "Makes sense, right? The worlds are all perfectly balanced, but when the walls begin breaking down, the stories start to crumble and strange things happen."

I glanced at him. "You kinda sound like you know what you're talking about."

Jack laughed. "I'm making it all up. But it does kind of make sense, right?"

My gaze wandered back to the stone in my hand, especially its flickering purple side. Something about it bugged me. "Maybe, the more tears and thinning borders and breakages within the story, the closer the source is," I muttered.

"What?"

"Like, the closer Glorathy is, the more the stories are fracturing."

"Right you are, girl!" came a familiar cackle as the air in front of Jack and I sparked with purple light and Glorathy appeared. Her staff seemed to glow even brighter than it had the first time I had seen her.

Copper growled and snapped at her, but had the sense to stay back.

"Hello there, Cassidy," Glorathy said, grinning to show a mouth full of yellow teeth. "We finally meet again! It's been so long!"

I glared at her. She had stolen my family and now had the nerve to show up and act like we were just old friends. She was making fun of me!

"I'm sure you're wondering where your nuisance of a father and his annoying daughter are," Glorathy said, addressing me, as if we were the only ones there.

I gritted my teeth together and nodded. "Tell me where you took my family. At least let me see them."

"Patience, patience," Glorathy said, twirling her staff in front of her like a baton, "It will all make sense soon."

"What are you doing this for?" I asked. "Why?"

Glorathy cackled so loudly that it bounced off the cliffs nearby and echoed around us.

Abruptly, Glorathy stopped and snapped her fingers. A notepad and pen appeared in her hands. "Always have evil villain monologue near cliffs, so maniacal laughter echoes around," she muttered as she scribbled away. "Noted." She tossed the notepad behind her and it vanished in a puff of purple smoke before it could touch the ground.

Floating slightly above the dusty earth, Glorathy approached Jack and I.

"Stay away," I ordered.

Glorathy laughed like it was the funniest thing she had ever heard. "Did you hear that? She's – you – I just can't – why -" She broke off, doubling over with laughter.

Jack and I exchanged a glance. Okay, so maybe my words meant nothing to her, but it wasn't as comical as Glorathy was making it out to be.

When Glorathy finished laughing, she stopped and cleared her throat. "Anyway, there's something I came here to do."

"Was it float around and spill your evil plan to us like all evil geniuses do?" I asked.

Glorathy placed a hand on her heart, like she was touched. "Thank you, for calling me a genius. It's a fact not many people seem to get. But the answer to your question is no. Been there, done that. It was super fun! The humans in your world are such crybabies! They freak out about one measly dragon!" She cackled again.

I froze, scenes of my hometown burning flashing in my mind; the hills on fire, the whole city going up in flames. And what had happened to the Hungry Caterpillar? And what about Danger and Trouble? Where were they? What else had escaped from the fictional world?

"I thought you were anti-friends, Cassie?" Glorathy asked, snapping me out of my thoughts. She was looking pointedly at Jack.

I folded my arms dismissively. "You don't know anything!"

Glorathy gave a creepy grin. "I've been watching you, Cassie. I know you better then you know yourself."

"Jack's my ally, that's different. We're only helping each other because we have aligned goals." Was I even convincing myself?

Glorathy snorted a laugh. "Really? I see. Well, this'll be fun." She raised her staff.

I braced myself for a flash of light, thinking she was going to disappear. Instead, two sealed tubes of glass slid up from the ground, looking very out of place beneath the huge rock.

"What are you doing?" I asked guardedly.

Glorathy let out another cackle of laughter. "Something fun... very, very fun."

I knew she'd be up to no good, but I wasn't prepared for what happened next. Reaching down with her staff, Glorathy smacked the end of it against the ground. A ripple ran through the dirt and a trail of purple sparks headed directly towards Copper and Jack. When it reached them, they disappeared. There was a flash as they reappeared, one in each glass tube. I panicked, racing over to Copper and banging on the glass. Picking up a fist-sized rock, I bashed it against the tube, but the glass was too strong and didn't shatter.

"Let them out!" I shouted, whirling on Glorathy.

Glorathy just laughed. "I think it's time you learned something about yourself, Cassidy Undering." She twirled her staff around above her head and there was a splashing sound. At first, it seemed like nothing happened. Then I watched with horror as water began rising inside the two twin glass tubes.

Jack spotted it too and looked up frantically to meet my gaze. He looked really scared.

Fury and desperation overruled my common sense. I charged at Glorathy, my rock in hand, prepared to attack. But before I even got close, purple sparks surrounded me, pushing me backwards and prying the rock out of my hand.

Glorathy laughed. "You really think you can attack me?"

I growled in frustration and glanced back over at the glass tubes. The water was already a few centimeters deep, wetting Jack's shoes, and was rising quickly. My gaze flashed over to Copper. He was attempting in vain to shake the water off his paws as it rose higher.

"Cassie, something you don't seem to realize is that allies don't usually stay allies for long," Glorathy said, pacing back and forth slowly in front of me. "Either, they fight and one defeats the other – well, that's my experience anyway – or they become… friends."

"I don't care," I said stubbornly, narrowing my eyes at Glorathy, "What are you trying to do?"

"You don't care? You don't care about him, huh?" Glorathy said, raising an eyebrow and twirling her staff to face me, "Well, this should be very easy, then."

The water had now reached Jack's waist and he was pounding on the glass, yelling something. The tubes were soundproof because I couldn't hear what he was saying. Copper was paddling now to keep afloat. His adorable puppy eyes were fixed on me, asking me to do something, but I was at an agonizing loss. I felt powerless.

"Now, Cassie," Glorathy said, turning to me as the water started soaking Jack's shirt. "I thought you had a difficult choice ahead. But, because you don't care about Jack, you should be fine. Just choose to eliminate him and your dog can go free."

I froze. I couldn't move, couldn't think, couldn't breathe. All in that moment, I realized the reality of my choice. I couldn't fight her.

Either Jack or Copper was going to die. That's what she wanted, an impossible choice.

Jack seemed to realize it too and he held my gaze, his green eyes desperate.

Jack or Copper.

Jack or Copper.

Jack.

Or Copper.

"What will it be, Cassie?" Glorathy intoned in a sing-song voice, "What's taking you so long? I thought you had already made up your mind. You don't want both of them to die do you?"

I ground my teeth together and tried to ignore her. The same words kept thumping in my head.

Jack.

Copper.

It should be easy. I didn't care about Jack. I didn't! He was a fictional character and I was just here to save my family. So why was my heart racing? Why couldn't I make the choice?

The water was now creeping over Jack's shoulders. Copper's little paws were paddling fast to keep above the water.

"Tell you what," Glorathy said, "This will be nice." She whirled her staff through the air, sending purple sparks raining down in front of me. Two shiny silver buttons that looked like they came out of a game show appeared on the ground, colourful and bizarre against their bland background.

"All you have to do is press one of these buttons," Glorathy said. "You won't even have to say it to his face when you eliminate him."

My eyes widened as I looked between the two buttons, one labeled Jack, the other labeled Copper. My gaze flashed back to Glorathy and I pleaded, "Let them out! Please! I'll do anything you want."

Glorathy just smiled an evil smile. "What I want, is for you to make a choice. Tick tock…"

I glared up at her. "You're a monster," I hissed.

Glorathy grinned. "Maybe so….. I'd suggest you hurry."

I glanced back at the traps to find that they were both completely full. Jack's eyes were wide as he clearly struggled to hold his breath. Copper's fur looked extra silky underwater. He frantically thrashed around, searching for a way out.

My dog, whom I'd had since he was a tiny puppy and loved so very much. Who had always been there to comfort me when I was sad and celebrate with me when I was happy. My best friend. It was an easy choice.

But Jack…

I shut my eyes and took a deep breath. It didn't help that Glorathy had decided to start making ticking noises in the background.

My eyes snapped open and I stepped onto a button. One of the glass cases shattered. The other didn't. It just retracted into the ground, leaving nothing but water...and a few scraps of fur.

Jack lay in a puddle of water and glass, gasping for breath. And Copper...

Copper was gone.

Glorathy smirked. "Interesting. I look forward to seeing you on the other side, Cassie." She vanished, leaving a swirling purple portal in her wake.

I didn't care. I crawled over to the puddle where my dog had been and cried.

I had let my best friend die.

CHAPTER TEN
Friends

Curled up at the bottom of the huge rock, I could think of nothing but how weird it felt, not having Copper with me. Whenever I was sad, Copper had always comforted me. He was always there. And now he wasn't.

I didn't have any tears left. Instead, I just stared as the puddle of water where I had last seen my puppy gradually soaked away into the dirt. Jack stood nearby. I could feel him looking at me. I couldn't bear to glance over at him.

Why had I done it?

Why had I saved Jack instead of Copper?

In my brain, it seemed crazy. But the answer was there. Jack was my friend and people were more important than pets. Even Copper. As I thought it, it felt so wrong. But I knew it was right.

As I thought about this, something hit me.

A flashback. A memory. Or a vision of some kind, because I could see myself in the memory.

There I was, unruly brown hair and sparkling dark brown eyes. I must have only been four or five. Where had that spark gone? My mother leaned over the tiny version of me, her blue eyes glistened and her curtain of hair falling around us. "Mummy is going away for a while, little one," my mother said.

"Where?" my tiny self asked, "Why?"

"I'm traveling," my mother replied, a glint in her eyes, "to capture a kangaroo from Australia and bring it back to you."

"Woah," tiny Cassie breathed, eyes wide. "Is Australia far away?"

My mother smiled. "Yes, little one, but don't worry. When I get back, it'll be like I was never gone."

"Can't you take me with you?" my little self pleaded.

"No little one, I can't," my mother said, "but I'll be thinking about you and Chloe the whole time and wishing I was already home."

"Are you getting Chloe a kang-i-roo too?"

"If she wants one," my mother said with a wink, laughing.

My dad's voice came from outside. "Come on, Emma! You're going to miss your flight."

My tiny self's eyes filled with tears. "Do you have to go?"

My mother wrapped her arms around my smaller self and nodded. "I do, Cassie. I'm sorry. Promise me one thing, sweet girl," she said, pulling back to look me in the eyes. "Don't lose your sparkle. Stay bright and bubbly and cheerful for me, okay?"

Little Cassie nodded and wiped her eyes.

"And one more thing," my mom said. "Remember, if you see someone down in the dumps, give them a smile. You can change the world for good by the little things you do. Let your light shine."

Mini Cassie nodded again. "Yes, Mummy."

My mother gave little me another tight squeeze. "I love you, little one. I'll be back before you know it."

Then she was gone, whirling outside in a flash of golden brown hair and a bright smile.

I realized my eyes were wet with tears again. I remembered the time my mother had gone on a business trip to Australia. It had been the worst month of my little life, without her. But I had kept smiling, kept laughing, kept a cheerful look on my face and a bubbly feeling in my heart. Because my mum had asked me to. She had always told me that I could change someone's day if I just shared a smile, or a kind word.

The tears welled up again, but I didn't let them spill over.

All this time, while I had been trying to shut people out and push others away; All this time, I had been doing exactly the opposite of what my mum would have wanted! I shut myself in the dark, instead of being a light and helping others.

I pictured dragons and giants wreaking havoc in New Zealand, then traveling over or under the sea to other countries. I pictured the walls of the fictional worlds breaking down completely, releasing every single storybook villain and monster into the real world. My world.

I lifted my head, a new feeling of determination inside me. In this life, people got hurt and people died. I couldn't do anything about it, and I couldn't stop myself from caring either. But I might be able to do something about this.

I had to stop Glorathy.

"Come on Jack," I said, standing up and turning to him with a grim expression on my face.

Jack looked at me, his eyes wide. He was still shaken by his near death experience. He raised an eyebrow. "What are you planning on doing?"

"We have to find Glorathy," I said. "I want to save my family. But I also have to get her to close the portals to the real world and return the fictional world to normal."

"So now you care what happens to other people?" Jack asked, raising an eyebrow and giving a slight smirk.

I rolled my eyes and gazed over at the portal Glorathy had left behind. "No matter how hard I try, I can't stop myself from caring about others. That's just what people do I guess. Lets go and save them."

I half expected Jack to say I was crazy thinking I could defeat a powerful sorceress like Glorathy. I expected him to wish me luck and leave, but he just grinned. "I'm in. What's the plan?"

"It seems like all her power is in the staff," I said. "So if we can get it, we could... I dunno, turn her into a frog or something."

Jack wrinkled his nose. "What about a cow instead? Sturdy, reliable, more useful."

I raised an eyebrow. "You really want Glorathy Dodge for your cow? She definitely wouldn't give you any milk."

Jack shrugged. "Hey, it was just an idea. More importantly, how do we get her staff in the first place?"

The cogs in my brain whirred as I tried to think of a plan. "Well, we'd need some sort of distraction. I could distract her and you sneak around and get her staff. We'll have to refine the plan when we see where she is."

Jack met my gaze. "Are you sure that will work?"

"Nope, not sure at all."

Jack glanced up at the portal, then back at me. "What's the plan if we get caught?"

I grinned. "Just wing it....and try not to die," I said with more confidence than I felt.

With one last glance at where the puddle had been, I strode towards the cloudy portal. Jack followed, stepping around the last of the water.

"Are you sure you want to come with me?" I asked. "It might get gnarly. You don't have to do this."

"This might sound really cliché," Jack replied, "but I'm with you. That's what friends are for."

I nodded. "Sure. Friends."

We linked hands and I glanced up at the portal. Before I had a chance to hesitate, Jack dove in headfirst, yanking me after him.

We landed at the top of a hill. I tumbled down the slope a little way before managing to stretch out a leg to stop myself. Standing up, I brushed off the grass and mud. Jack was sitting up further down the mound. Rubbing the hip that I had landed on, I tromped up to the top of the hill and gazed around.

This world seemed different to the others I had been in. It seemed more... simplistic. Bland, in a way. A bit like the village and villagers in Snow White's world, but worse. Sure, the grass I was standing on was green, but it seemed like only two shades of green, a bit like a child's drawing. Plus, it barely rustled in the breeze I could feel in my hair. Neither did the leaves on the trees nearby, which looked just as plain and un-textured. It was as if the writer of the story hadn't spent enough time describing their scenery.

Speaking of the story, what was this one?

As if he had heard me, Jack asked, "Do you recognize this story?" He had tramped up to stand next to me at the top of the hill.

I shook my head. "Nah. Could be any badly written novel. I have no clue where Glorathy is, but she left that portal open, so she's probably prepared for us."

"She didn't know how long it would take us though," Jack pointed out.

I nodded. "True. What do we do now? How do we find her? She must have gone to this world for a reason......I guess we just pick a direction and see if we can find someone to ask about Glorathy."

Jack agreed, pointing out some houses a little way away, and we set off down the hill again, walking this time. After passing several sketchy looking houses, sketchy in multiple ways, we came to a bridge. The bridge was the first thing I had seen in this world so far that didn't look like you could cut it up with a pair of scissors. The writer must have spent at least some time making it appear in the reader's mind. Why? What was special about it?

"There's a sign here," Jack said as we approached the bridge.

The wooden bridge was wide, wide enough for two horses to pass each other with some breathing room. It spanned a rushing river, which appeared to flow green, but with the pencil drawn look of it, I wasn't one hundred percent sure.

While Jack read the sign, I twirled a lock of my hair absentmindedly between my fingers and, with a jolt, realized it was still blue. With everything that had happened already in the past while, I had forgotten about the witch's spell. I wondered vaguely how long it would last.

"Cassie, come look at this," Jack said.

I wandered over and squinted at the tiny white letters on the sign. "BEWARE the bridge of doom, for behind it lies TROUBLE and under it you will meet DANGER," I read aloud, my confusion growing with every word, "What?"

"Exactly what I thought," Jack said.

I glanced at the bridge. "Doesn't really look very dangerous. It's just a bridge, and nobody is there."

Bending down, Jack peered underneath, but shook his head. "Nothing under it."

"Beware! Trouble! She coming! Danger!" came a voice that sounded familiar.

My eyes widened. "Danger?" I called out.

From behind one of the badly drawn trees, the little monster appeared, his purple eyes wide. I might have imagined it, but I thought he looked happy to see me.

"Danger!" he called out, waddling over to Jack and I. Another familiar face followed him. The pale-furred creature with the long neck, and giraffe-like head was easily recognizable, especially when he blinked his huge orange eyes and gave a toothy grin. His fluffy squirrel-like tail swept over the ground behind him.

"Bothering bingbats, if it ain't dat girl from da purple cloud thingee!" Trouble exclaimed. "Ain't never espected ta see da likes 'a you round 'ere!"

"Beware!" Danger cried.

At that, another little monster appeared. This one was also the elongated shape of a rugby ball, with darker gray fur than Trouble, but not quite as dark as Danger. This creature had only one eye, although it was huge. It was an ocean blue colour, not unlike my hair.

"This one be Beware!" Trouble introduced the newcomer, "He don't talk like, but he ain't dangerus."

Beware opened his tiny mouth, revealing two minuscule fangs. All that came out was a sort of 'blarf' noise.

"Danger! She coming! Beware, beware!" Danger warbled.

Trouble rolled his huge eyes. "She's-a already come, ya digger'oop! Ya don' need ta keep ya chant up now!"

"Danger!" Danger yipped.

"Shut yer mouth afore ya gets us caught by Wurrles!" Trouble snapped. "Yer dense as a dingledong, Danger!"

"This is Jack," I said. "My... friend. He and I are here to find Glorathy."

"Beware!" Danger cried out.

"Blart!" Beware gurgled.

"What are you guys doing here?" I asked.

"This be our 'ome! Me, Danger an' Beware! We lives hereabouts, like. This be our bridge."

"Really?" I said. "This is your story?"

"And hers," Trouble said solemnly, his orange serious, "She be watchin', waitin' round every corner. Enawhere an' everywhere. No one be safe."

I froze.

"This is Glorathy's story?" Jack beat me to my question.

All three little monsters nodded.

"Danger," Danger whispered. "She coming."

"Blurg!" Beware snorted. "Blarf!"

"We're trying to find her," I told them, feeling a mixture of relief and stress that we were finally getting close, "Can you help us?"

Beware waddled in a distressed circle, his single turquoise eye wide. "Blart! Shoof!"

"Daaaanger!" Danger said, his purple eyes widening.

Trouble pondered the question. Beware shook his "head" vigorously, which looked very comical. His arms jerked around limply as his body whirled to create the motion of shaking his "head". But Trouble was thinking.

"She can git to us enawhere enaway," Trouble reasoned, "We's alredy been pushed and pulled like, all over the place in them purple cloud thingees."

Beware paused his twisting to frown. "Blarf! Blooge! Binggle!"

"We'll be helpin' ya," Trouble announced.

"Thank you," I said, smiling.

Trouble just shook his head. "Don't be thankin' us yet. Yer still goin'a have ta get there afore the Wurrles get to us."

"What's a Wurrle?" I asked.

Beware stretched his little arms out as wide as they would go. "Blart," he said, looking very serious.

"Giant versions of us Ruggles, wi' half the brains and fi'ty times the evil," Trouble told her.

"Danger!" Danger called.

Trouble rolled his eyes again. "Danger means that we ain't sure what they're up to. One of em is 'eaded this way though, the Doggle'ops warned us. They seen im comin'."

"Then we need to hurry," I said, shuddering at the thought of facing another giant version of Danger.

"Yer right about that!" Trouble agreed, giving a grin, "Off we 'a go! Dinna dawdle! Don't wan'ta become a Wurrle's meal."

He began waddling off across the bridge. Danger trotted after him. After a moment, Beware seemed to realize they had already left and hurried after them. I exchanged a glance with Jack, then shrugged and followed the Ruggles.

We passed through badly drawn forest, occasionally broken up by vague, undefined lakes and sluggish rivers. The ground remained flat, without even a bump or stray stone on the path we were following. Occasionally, I spotted the same rifts we had seen in the Swiss Family Robinson book. Purple light glittered around the edges, as they slowly grew wider. Time was running out.

After walking for a while, we came to a hill. The path remained perfectly smooth as we tramped uphill behind Trouble and the others.

I zoned out for most of the walk until I felt something brushing my ankle. Glancing down, I saw that Danger had dropped back from Trouble and Beware to walk next to me. As I looked down, he gazed up at me with huge purple eyes. "Coppa?" he said. He glanced around, as if checking, then looked back at me. "Coppa?" he asked again.

I looked away as tears pricked in my eyes. I wouldn't cry. Not again. I was going to defeat Glorathy. For Copper.

For Mum.

For everyone else, in the real world and the fictional one.

"Copper's gone, Danger," I told the little creature.

Danger's eyes, already so round, grew wider. "Coppa?"

"No Copper," I told him, shaking my head, "But I'm going to make Glorathy pay."

"Beware," Danger said, his huge eyes watery. "She power. Trouble." Then he waddled away to catch up with his fellow Ruggles.

As we continued, I noticed that the ground seemed to be trembling. After a while, I thought I could hear a distant thudding.

Thud.

Thunk.

Thud.

Thunk.

It sounded almost like... footsteps.

"Is that the... Wurrle?" I asked.

"That'd be it, alright!" Trouble announced not even stopping.

"Blarf!" Beware jumped about wildly, his eye wide, his arms flailing.

"Oh, hold yer hoofalings, Beware!" Trouble muttered, "It ain't caught us yet. Faster, ya dooglebuds! Can't be caught now!"

We hurried on as fast as we could, but the thing with the Wurrles being larger, it also meant they were faster. The thudding got louder and with each thud came a quake that nearly shook me off my feet. Beware and Danger were running as fast as they could on their stubby little legs, but every time the ground shook they kept tumbling over, popping up into the air like popcorn and rolling over backwards, slowing our progress. Eventually, Jack picked up Danger and I scooped up Beware and we kept running after Trouble.

"Yer lookin' fer a big hole, like! A cave! Should be just o'er the next rise!" Trouble called as we sprinted.

"Bloggle!" Beware said, "Shcoof!"

Once we reached the top of the hill, we paused to breathe and I glanced back. Freezing, I nearly toppled over. My jaw dropped until I was sure it was dragging on the ground.

I could see the Wurrle now. It was huge, much larger than the one that had invaded Snow

White's story. It was a massive furry rugby ball in a dull shade of gray. Its body was at least as big as a dump truck and its arms and legs were as thick as tree trunks. Even from far away, I could tell it wasn't as well described in this story as the Ruggles. Its fur seemed scribbly rather than soft. The eyes were not huge in their bodies like Danger's. Instead, they were barely visible in the Wurrle's fur.

"Wurrles ne'er can see good," Trouble commented, "Prob'ly them tiny eyes, but I ne'er asked, like."

"We should go," Jack said, as the Wurrle slowly thundered closer.

"Yer right about that," Trouble said, "Git moving! Keep yer eyes peeled fer Glorathy's hole."

We raced on. Every thud of the Wurrle's footsteps reminded me of the imminent danger we were in. In my arms, Beware was trembling. The little creature seemed to be terrified.

As we passed fields of scribbly grass and dull, slow-moving rivers, I vaguely wondered what Glorathy's story was. When she had first appeared in my world, she had mentioned being neglected. She had mentioned her story being passed up for others. Being in it now, I could kind of understand why. But was that really the only reason she was doing this? Was that why she wanted to destroy the non-fictional world? Revenge for being ignored?

Before I could ponder this too much, Beware squirmed upright in my arms and pointed with one noodle-like arm. "Blart! Blooge!"

I stopped and followed his finger to where he was pointing. There was a huge rift, much larger than any I had seen before. Something moved in the blurry space, but it was still too fuzzy to see what it was through the opaque, thinninging border between the worlds.

"Yeah, it's a rift between the worlds, Beware," I told the creature.

Beware rolled his eye and wriggled out of my grasp. Plopping onto the ground, he stood up and waddled over to where he'd been pointing. Behind the rift, there was a dark hole in the ground. It was nearly invisible behind the shiny purple patch of the rift.

"My jimmy-joppers!" Trouble exclaimed, "I'd a never spott'd that meself!"

"Danger!" Danger cried out, alarm in his tone.

Boom!

The earth jolted so much it threw even Jack and I onto the ground. A dark shadow loomed over us. I dreaded what I was about to see.

"Snarf!" the Wurrle said, snapping at us.

"We're doomed," I muttered.

CHAPTER ELEVEN
Battles Ahead

The Wurrle growled again and a huge paw swept towards us. I scooped Beware back up and dove to the side to avoid it. Jack leapt the other way. Trouble ducked behind a tree to hide.

"We 'ave ta knock 'em over!" Trouble called out. "Den 'e won't be much of a botha'. It be heavy at the top, like, an' dey 'ave trouble gettin' up ag'in."

"Got it," Jack said, dodging another heavy blow that made the ground shake.

Not sure if Trouble knew what he was talking about, I placed Beware on the ground and quickly analyzed the huge beast. We were never going to be able to knock it over from down on the ground. Not unless we had a huge tripwire or a piece of rope. Which we didn't. So we had to somehow knock it over without being able to trip it up.

Yanking my bow off my back, I aimed for the monster's eye, but it whirled around at the last second and my arrow only bounced harmlessly off its back. Reaching for another arrow, I realized that it was the last one. I had to hit my shot or I was out of easy options. I lined up my aim. I held my breath. I released the arrow. It flew directly towards the Wurrle's mouth as it roared at us. My hopes rose, and then were crushed as the huge beast lifted its hand and swatted the arrow away.

That was that.

I was out of ideas.

"Ya got enathing else up yer sleeves?" Trouble shouted as the Wurrle swung its entire body towards me, seeking the source of where the arrows had come from and growling menacingly.

"No!" I told him as I darted out of the monster's line of sight.

"We need a plan!" Jack called out as the creature swiped a hand towards him and he dive-rolled out of the way.

My gaze strayed to the monster's legs, as it stomped around trying to locate us again. Unlike the limbs of the three Ruggles, which were smooth, the legs of the Wurrle were lumpy and ridged, like a child's scribble. The fur of its torso was also coarse and rough. It reminded me of the climbing walls I'd scrambled up when I was younger. With an idea forming in my mind, I met Jack's gaze.

"Distract it for me," I told him.

"Er..Okay, what are you going to do?" Jack asked.

"I'm going up," I said, flexing my fingers and arms.

Before Jack could ask how, the Wurrle's hand came down again and we leapt apart to avoid it. Jack nodded to me, then darted out into the Wurrle's line of sight.

"Hey!" he shouted. "Big furry idiot!"

As the lumbering Wurrle snarled at Jack, I raced up to its leg. The bumps and ridges on the surface of its leg were just like the rocky crags I was used to climbing in the Port Hills. My fingers easily found the little crevices and cracks to grab as I swiftly clambered up the thick leg. The creature didn't seem to notice me. It swung at Jack again and he dodged out of the way, his gaze flickering to me as I struggled to hang on as the huge beast moved. I continued up the leg and reached around the overhang of the Wurrle's belly to grasp a tuft of thick fur. Feeling partially terrified and partially hopeful, I pulled myself up, hand over hand, until I was face to face with the Wurrle.

It was mad.

Its little black eyes, practically buried in fur, widened and it snarled. I shifted my grip a little as it snapped at me, jerking its head wildly.

"Cassie, be careful!" Jack called.

Hanging on for dear life with one hand, I drew back my other arm, my fist clenched, and socked the monster in the eyeball. Hard. It flinched and wobbled. Letting out a loud groan, it reached up with both giant hands and swatted me away. I plummeted the few metres to the ground, landing on my feet and rolling to avoid the impact. The Wurrle squinted its tiny eyes, blinked, then squinted again. Its eye appeared to be leaking some kind of fluid. Slowly, it turned, growling, and tromped away down the hill, the ground shaking even after it was out of sight.

"Ya did a fine job 'a that!" Trouble announced jubilantly, as he came out from behind the tree. "Think ya best 'a be goin' in now, though. Ain't got much time left."

I glanced at him. "You're not coming?"

"Da big boss lady, er, she be in 'ere," Trouble said, pointing to the hole, "Ain't no way I'ma goin in."

"Danger..." Danger agreed, although he looked apologetic as he reached up to hand me one of the arrows that I had shot,.

"Blart!" Beware cried out, waddling in a circle.

"Well....thanks for your help," I said, "See you on the other side."

Trouble nodded. "Sure girl," he said and suddenly looked sad. "Blithering bozzlehops! If ya make it back, then dizzlegobs can fly! Still, appreciate yer enthusiasm. Good luck. Ye'll need it."

My footsteps felt heavy as I made my way down a long passageway that sloped steadily downwards. The floor was smooth and the walls were stone, though they seemed to be only one single colour, with zero shading. Glorathy's story definitely had a budget feel.

Partway down, Jack stopped walking and glanced over at me. "So... refining the plan?"

I shrugged. How do you defeat someone who has so much power? "Bust in and demand Glorathy give up?"

Jack laughed. "For some reason, I don't think that'll work. We need a proper plan, Cassie. She's very powerful. We have to outsmart her somehow. Maybe distracting her and grabbing the staff would work, but it might be hard to distract her. What was your plan before? You know, before everything... that's happened."

I looked away. "I... uh... didn't have one."

I could feel Jack staring. "You're telling me that you jumped into a potentially dangerous portal to face a very powerful sorceress and you didn't have a plan at all? I thought there might be some fancy gadget from your world that could help us."

I shook my head. "I wasn't really thinking about how I would save my family, I just knew I couldn't do nothing!" It seemed stupid now, especially considering what had happened to Copper.

"Sounds like you didn't really think at all," Jack commented. I shoved him and he grinned. "What? It's true! Who goes to face an evil magic lady without a plan?"

"Maybe you're right, but that's not going to help us now," I said, getting serious, "We do need a better plan."

"Wow, what a great idea," Jack deadpanned, rolling his eyes.

I was tempted to shove him again. "How about I use this?" I pulled the bow off my back and started walking again.

"You're going to shoot Glorathy?" Jack asked incredulously.

"Just...like, threaten her," I said. "So she reverses the portals and stuff.....and then sends us home." I didn't know what else to do, I was just desperate.

"Just like that?" Jack asked, disbelieving.

"Just like..." I trailed off. We had come to a door of sorts. It was crudely made out of what appeared to be random pieces of wood. In spite of our lack of any real plan and the imminent danger, Jack did not desert me.

"Reckon this is it?" Jack asked nervously, reaching up to grab the handle.

I nodded. "Let's go."

It opened surprisingly easily and without a sound. Quietly, we squeezed through.

And there she was. Glorathy Dodge, dressed in a different robe to the last time we had seen her, though this one was still just as dull. Her gray hair was as unruly as ever. She had her back to us and appeared to be concentrating on her staff, which seemed to be covered in strands of algae, though it was hard to say for sure in the dim light.

"Oh! Cassie! Jack!" Glorathy spun around and frowned. "You're early! I had this whole entrance planned and..." she sighed, "Oh well. Anyway, welcome to my book! What do you think of the place?"

I glanced around, wrinkling my nose at the smell, which was like someone had left dozens of rotting fish lying around. For the most part, the cave we were in was a lot like the rest of this story world, vague, plain and bland. There were some details, like the algae hanging from the ceiling and the texture of the dirt floor, but other than that it was pretty boring. To our left, there was a huge crevasse, deep enough to make me shudder.

Glorathy frowned. "I know, I know, the author of this book was rather lacking in descriptive talents. This cave used to belong to a swarm of gnat-squid, annoying little things. Took ages to clear them out." She delicately pulled a strand of algae off her staff and tossed it into the crevasse.

"What made you think I would come?" I asked, somewhat mystified about what she actually wanted and buying us some time, "You seemed pretty determined to stop us last time we met."

Glorathy laughed. "Cassidy Ella Undering, I thought you were smarter. You see, my dear girly, the key word in that sentence is 'seemed'. I knew from the start you wouldn't give up. I knew you would be perfect for my plan."

Jack and I exchanged a glance. "What plan?" we asked simultaneously.

Glorathy cackled again. "You haven't figured it out?" She asked in mock surprise. She sighed and turned away from us, gazing up at the ceiling. "You see, my story was written only a few years ago. It was in bookstores and available online. My ignorant clod of a writer tried everything to get my book to sell, apart from writing an interesting book that is! But it didn't sell. At all! You pesky readers chose other books over mine.....and it was infuriating! How could I be overlooked. Me, the most powerful, beautiful, glorious sorceress ever to be created! How can I be so incredibly powerful, yet not have been noticed at all? So I devised a plan. It took years to gain enough power to escape my book, but I had the time and the patience. I planned to write my own story, not have someone else dictate my every move! Make a story that everyone would want to read. But it's not a book – it's real! I was the perfect villain, all I needed was a courageous hero. And there you were Cassie, ripe for the taking, so serious and oh so protective of your dear, if somewhat dim, father and sister"

"That's why you took my family?" I asked, eyes widening. "So you could create a story? That makes no sense. You only found me because of a mistake. I heard you say you wanted your portal to take you to Auckland."

Glorathy waved her staff offhandedly. "Details, details. It all worked out in the end. You got to go on a long adventurous journey, and I get the attention that I deserve."

I stared at her. "You created a billion portals, invaded my world, and stole my family... just so you could be famous?"

Glorathy grinned. "Smart girl, Cassie. That's exactly right."

"So what are you going to do now?" I asked. "You know the hero always wins, right?"

Glorathy's grin widened. "Not in my story." She struck the floor with her staff and I fell into darkness.

Blinking, I shoved myself up from the floor. Except it wasn't a floor anymore. I gasped as I realized I was now on a plank of wood swinging over a huge drop to a smooth expanse of water below. I looked up to find that the ropes I was hanging from extended up into the clouds. There was no sign of land anywhere near. And there was no sign of Glorathy or Jack. Had Glorathy teleported me? Why was I here? Where was here? The platform I sat on swung as a mild breeze brushed past.

I sucked in a breath and looked down. The height made me feel light-headed. I backed up a little, leaning back on my hands, but retracted my hand as they hit nothing but air behind me. I shuffled so I was back in the middle of the plank. Another gust of wind whirled past, shoving the platform as if urging it to come and play.

Clinging to the wood, I tried to search for a way out. A path of escape. There was nothing. Nothing but the air around me and the water below me. I couldn't help but glance down again and the water seemed to grow farther and farther away, lengthening the massive drop. My breath came in short, uneven gasps. My eyes were wide. Now a huge blast of wind abruptly shook the plank, nearly knocking me off. I hung on for dear life as another gale-force gust swirled around me. As if of its own accord, the plank started to tip. I tried to steady it, but the wind wrecked my balance. With one mammoth gust, the breeze swept me off the wood and into the air.

For a moment, I seemed to hang in midair, like the way a cartoon character would before falling. Then came the drop. Wind whipped past me, blowing my ocean blue hair into my face as I plummeted. My stomach dropped and I let out a scream, which whirled away on the breeze. I squeezed my eyes shut and waited for the inevitable smack as I hit the water, praying this whole thing was a dream.

But I stopped falling.

Opening my eyes, I blinked as I now found myself lying face down in an ordinary meadow, the grass tickled my face and the sky above was so bright blue that it seemed nearly fake. It seemed too good to be true. Swiftly I checked myself all over, feeling for broken bones, as if I could have just blacked out for the landing and somehow ended up here. But there was no pain. No wounds. Nothing abnormal except for the bedraggled strands of teal hair hanging down into my face because my ponytail had come undone.

With my heart still beating a hundred miles per hour, my gaze flicked around, taking in my new surroundings, scanning for potential dangers. What was going on? First the platform above the ocean and now this?

The meadow seemed fairly safe, so I slowly stood up. As I did, I heard a familiar cackle. There was a flash of light, and the sky turned dark and foreboding. The grass became hard dirt underneath my feet and my shoes became covered in a dark flowing substance. A salty, metallic stench floated up to reach my nostrils and I froze. Blood. It came from behind me.

My head whipped around to see where all the blood was coming from and I opened my mouth to scream, but I couldn't make a sound. There, lying partway up a rise, struggling weakly on the dirt with blood flowing down the hill all around them, were Chloe and Dad.

"Save us, Cassie!" Chloe cried out, her gaze fixed on me, "Help us!"

I tried to run to them, but my legs wouldn't move through the sludgy red liquid, which somehow seemed thicker than blood. What had Glorathy done to them?

"I'm here! I'm coming!" I tried to shout, but again my mouth made no sound.

The flood of sticky liquid flowed over my family, as I struggled towards them. I reached out to them, but I was too far away. Their faces, panicked gazes fixed on me, disappeared last.

"No!" I screamed, but yet again, there was no sound. I fell to my knees in the thick liquid.

And then it disappeared. So did the meadow. I was now on the edge of a rocky cliff. I scrambled to my feet, surprised to feel that my clothes were clean and dry. Sure, they were still ragged from my story hopping, but no trace of blood remained. I was completely confused and distraught.

"Dad." My tears seeped out of my eyes. "Chloe." My heart was smashed into pieces. They were gone.

"Tut, tut, Cassie," came a familiar voice, "Crying?"

I whirled around to find Glorathy standing a few metres away. She was grinning at me. "We were having such fun weren't we?" she said.

I let out a roar; a roar that voiced all my rage, grief, and frustration. A dagger suddenly materialized in my hand and I charged at Glorathy. "You killed them!" The dagger sank into Glorathy's stomach. I stepped back and Glorathy fell to her knees, her eyes wide, clutching her stomach around the dagger.

"You..." Glorathy gasped, "You win..."

I was instantly mortified. I didn't feel like I had won. I dropped to my knees beside her, but it was too late, her glassy sightless eyes gazed up to the sky. Shaking her gently, I called her name, but I knew it was fruitless. Why was I even bothering? She had killed my family. She deserved this didn't she? So why did I feel like I had lost?

Glorathy's body began to spark purple, and as I watched, it slowly faded away. Then the cliff and the sky and the rocks began to fade too. I was too shocked to do anything as my surroundings faded into something very different.

Something familiar.

"There you are, Cass!" Chloe said, peeking around the corner into my room and grinning. "Come on, it's dinnertime!"

I just stared at her with wide eyes.

Chloe frowned at me. "Cassie? Are you okay?"

"I-" I stuttered. "I- uh...what?....uh, yeah, I'll come in a minute."

Chloe shrugged. "Okay. Don't take too long. Come on, Copper!"

Copper.

The little brown dog barked and leaped off my bed, following Chloe out of the room.

I stared after them. How was this happening? Had everything somehow been reversed? Was it possible that the whole thing had been some kind of dream? Maybe I had been asleep the whole time and there were really no portals, no Glorathy. I took a step forward and a strand of hair fell in front of my eyes. It was brown. Not teal, brown.

Had the whole thing really been a dream, then?

"Cassie!" came Dad's voice. He sounded happier than he had in years.

"Coming!" I called, trying to convince myself this was real. I exited my room and headed to the dining room. But in the doorway to the room, I froze. My eyes stretched wide and my whole body trembled.

"M- Mum?"

She turned to look at me, her blue eyes sparkling just as they once had, and smiled. "Yes, Cassie?"

I backed up a little. "Why- How- What kind of-"

"What is it, Cassie?" Chloe asked, scrunching up her brow in confusion, "You're acting really weird."

"How are you alive?" I asked my mother in a whisper. Not only alive, but she was well! Her golden brown hair shone and her skin glowed. It was the way she had been before. Before the cancer.

My mother laughed. "Alive? I've been alive for a long time, little one."

I shook my head as the cold, hard truth hit me. It was simply not possible. "None of this is real. You aren't real. You aren't-" I broke off as tears threatened to appear.

"What do you mean?" Dad asked, "Of course we're real."

But I knew that they were not. This was just a cruel hallucination that Glorathy had created. So, so cruel. Glorathy's voice filled my head.

You can stay here, she said, *You can live the life you never had because your mother died. You can really live.*

I hesitated. My mother was smiling at me, just the way she used to, as she patted the seat next to her.

"Come on Cass," she urged, "Tell me about school today….and archery. Did you make any new friends?"

I took a step towards her.

"I made your favourite," Dad told me, "Tuna pasta. I'll let you serve yourself first."

Even Copper was gazing at me from under the table where my feet were supposed to be. His beautiful eyes implored me to come, to give in to the temptation of a redo. A life with my mum. A perfect life. The one that had been stolen from me by the cancer. I took another step closer.

"Come on, little one," Mum said, "I'll even enroll you in that camp you wanted to go on."

All of a sudden, a memory flashed into my mind. My mother, telling me that I should always be nice to others. Telling me that I should make friends, take risks, and have fun. Because what was the point of living if I wasn't really living at all?

I had to care.

And I did.

I couldn't leave the rest of the world to die while I lived in a fake reality created by Glorathy. I owed it to Jack, to the people, and to my family – my real family – to at least try.

"No," I said loudly, with purpose and determination.

Chloe, Dad, Mum, and Copper all stared at me. It physically hurt to tear myself away from their gazes and race away, out of that house, slamming the door behind me. I heard my family calling after me but didn't look back. I shut my eyes as I ran. It had been hard, harder than anything I had ever done before, but I knew it was the right choice.

CHAPTER TWELVE
Fiction For Real

I knew that I was waking up for real this time because I was back in the cave with Jack shaking me by the shoulders and Glorathy screeching in the background. I bolted upright instantly, giving Jack barely a second to back off before I was up on my feet.

"You were supposed to be trapped forever!" Glorathy shouted. "You were supposed to stay in the worlds I created! Worlds under *my* control! You are such annoying little brats!"

I glared at her. Glancing at Jack, I vaguely wondered what his hallucinations had been about, but I didn't ask. Now was not the time. We had to get rid of Glorathy once and for all. But as I glanced down to where my bow and arrow lay, I couldn't make myself pick them up. Not only did I think that Glorathy would easily be able to stop me, but I knew in my heart that I couldn't kill her.

I couldn't do it.

Glorathy seemed to realize that both of us were looking at her and she stopped her tantrum to stare back at us. "How were you able to break out? How? I was sure this would work. Glory would be mine!" She seemed desperate and on edge, not really making total sense. But I figured that she was a badly written fictional character after all.

"Glory?" I questioned, "What you've done won't give you glory. It will only make people fear you and despise you."

Glorathy grinned. "Yes! Others fearing me gives me the power!"

"No," Jack interrupted, "it doesn't. When others fear you, it makes you unloved and unwanted."

Glorathy blinked at him, her gaze narrowing with fury. "What? What do you know, boy?"

"I know that nobody will like you now," Jack said.

"What you want is to be noticed, right?" I said, "Not to be feared. Fame does not have to be notoriety. You just think that one goes hand in hand with the other."

"If nobody will pay me any attention then they deserve to fear me!" Glorathy cackled. "I'm not listening to you children!" She raised her staff and purple clouds and sparks flashed in the air, swirling around the tip of her staff and causing Jack and I to duck as it roiled and thundered. The room grew dimmer and I crouched on the floor, gazing up at Glorathy's gradually growing storm cloud.

"You can be noticed without being feared!" I called out over the sound of thunder.

Glorathy didn't react, but I could tell she heard me.

I continued, "You've created a story, isn't that enough? You don't have to be a villain! You can save the day too!"

I may have been imagining it, but I thought the storm calmed a little. Jack watched me with wide eyes, as I met Glorathy's gray gaze through a haze of purple fog.

"*This* is your story," I said, "because I'm going to write it! You *can* be noticed. You can be known for changing your mind at the end and showing mercy! You can help us save the world!"

Glorathy's eyes narrowed. The storm gave an especially massive flash, but it seemed to grow a little smaller.

"Help us destroy the portals and get everyone back to their own worlds!" I urged, "You can do the right thing!"

Glorathy frowned. She seemed conflicted. Then she smashed her staff against the floor and I was flooded with purple light. When the light cleared, there were two slumped and dirty figures on the ground next to Glorathy. They were bedraggled and looked wary.

"Dad!" I cried out. "Chloe!"

Chloe looked up and her eyes lit up when she saw me. "Cassie!" She raced over and threw her arms around me. Dad followed soon after, wrapping his arms around both of us.

"Where have you been?" Chloe demanded, pulling back. "Where are we? And why do you have *blue* hair?"

"Teal," I corrected, twirling a strand between my fingers, "And it's a long story."

"As thrilling and heart-warming as this reunion is," Glorathy interrupted bluntly, "I have places to be and things to do. I'm sick of this."

I turned to the sorceress and glared at her. "You're going nowhere. You *don't* have anything to do." As I met Glorathy's cold gray gaze, something flickered there. Just a hint of doubt.

It was that speck of doubt that made the decision for me. When Glorathy raised her staff, creating a swirling purple portal in the air next to her, I leapt forward. Jack reacted a moment later, maybe guessing what I planned to do. But he was too late. Just as Glorathy disappeared into the portal, I jumped in after her and it sealed behind me.

This ride was different to the last few portal hops I had done. It felt shakier. Maybe it was the worlds collapsing, or maybe it was just me, but the purple void around me seemed to tremble. Everything flashed past in record time and I couldn't focus on anything. Then I landed.

The ground was hard, but I leapt up immediately and found Glorathy staring at me with a sickening grin.

"I knew you wouldn't be able to resist following me," Glorathy said, "You're a hero after all."

"I'm not a hero," I told her, "I'm a nobody."

Glorathy snorted. "Pathetic! Nobodies don't go on quests across the entire fictional world."

I shrugged. "You took my family. If you hadn't, I wouldn't have been worried about anything. I wouldn't have come after you. I wouldn't even have cared when the world was invaded."

Glorathy rolled her eyes in disdain. "Then why did you follow me? You got your family back, now you've left them again. What loyalty, what honour." She cackled. "What a *hero*," she said sarcastically.

I realized that she may be trying to stall, trying to distract me from what was going on. I glanced around, scanning my surroundings for an advantage. We were in a forest, that much I could tell, but the forest was being eaten up by the purple rifts. It seemed half forest, half ocean, and the air smelled like a peculiar mix of salt and mud and something rotten.

"You don't have to be the bad guy," I said, hardly realizing the words had come out of my mouth.

Glorathy rolled her eyes. "This again. I told you, the only villains who are remembered are the most evil ones. I was created this way. The most powerful sorceresses are always evil." She stamped her staff against the ground and the grass under my feet rippled enough that I toppled over.

"They don't have to be," I said, scrambling up. "You can be different!"

"Stop talking!" Glorathy shouted, smacking her staff on the ground again with fury.

"But it's true!" I persisted, managing to keep my balance as the ground rolled underneath me again.

"No, it's not!" Glorathy said.

In my mind, I could see what Glorathy was doing. She was refusing to believe that she was wrong. She didn't want to admit she could change. But the world was going to collapse if I didn't do something.

"Glorathy," I said. "You are the only one who can fix this. You can fix it all. You can be the *hero*, not the villain. I know you didn't want to go this far and make all the worlds collapse. You can still save everyone, and they would love it!"

Glorathy's gray eyes sparked with a intrigue. "But how would anybody know?"

"I'll write the story, like I said I would. A fictional character can't create a fictional story.

But I'm from the real world, so I can," I told her. "I can help you, you just have to help me."

Glorathy narrowed her eyes. "What would this story be about?"

I considered the question for a moment. "How about... a 'true' story about the time the fictional world was connected with the real world?"

Glorathy stroked her chin with her hand. I held my breath, hoping against hopes that it was enough. I had no doubt that without Glorathy's help, the worlds would surely collapse. I was relying completely on the person who'd caused this mess in the first place. I was relying on her to fix it.

"And you could have money," I said, "and a great place to live that's better than a damp old cave that used to belong to gnat-squids. I'll write it all."

Glorathy frowned. "It's not good enough!" Then she raised her staff and purple sparks went flying. But she was somewhat distracted and not very fast this time. I rushed forward and clasped the staff's handle as well, trying to get it off her.

We seemed to flicker between worlds as the tug of war over the staff continued. I thought I spotted the giants in their home for a second, then they were replaced by a picture of the Wicked Witch of the Compass helping farmers grow their crops. That flashed away just as quickly and Snow White appeared, speaking to her people from a high balcony in the castle. The images kept on flicking past and I held the staff as tightly as I could, trying to yank it out of Glorathy's hands. Some of the stories I recognized, others were too vague or unknown. At one point I thought I spotted the Ruggles, huddled outside the cave, anxiously waiting for us to return as the purple rift grew wider.

"Let… go… of… my… staff!" Glorathy shouted through gritted teeth.

My fingers were slippery but I held on and shook my head determinedly. "You have to help us get rid of the portals! They'll destroy the whole world!"

"Well, maybe I want the world to be destroyed!" Glorathy hissed, "They never cared about me anyway!"

"So you want them to die?" I asked, "Just because they never knew you existed? Besides, if the real world is destroyed, the fictional world would be destroyed too because it's created by the people in the real world!"

"I don't care if they die too! They deserve to after the way they treated me! They all deserve it!" Glorathy said. "Nobody ignores me, nobody!"

They clearly had. I figured pointing out that the fact people had ignored her was how we were in this mess, wasn't a great move, so I didn't. But I thought it. Then a thought struck me. Glorathy was lonely. And I could tell, because I had been lonely too.

I gave the staff one last final yank and said, "If you reversed the spells and fixed the portals, you'd be a hero. You'd have real friends."

That seemed to make everything freeze. The images stopped whirling around and we landed back in the cave. Chloe, Dad, and Jack all stared at us with wide eyes. I let go of the staff as Glorathy gazed at me with her eyes narrowed.

"What would you know about friendship?" she asked, "You claim not to care."

"But I did care," I said, "I couldn't stop caring. Friendship is when someone is willing to share their life with you or even give their life for you.

It's when someone cares enough to ask if you're okay. It's when someone cares enough that they stick by you, even when you don't want them to." As I spoke, I could sense Jack grinning.

Glorathy was silent for a long time. The silence was only broken up by my ragged panting as I struggled to catch my breath. After a few minutes of silence, Glorathy raised her staff again. I tensed, ready for her to strike. Instead, she lowered the magical stick and looked at me with intense gray eyes.

"You'll write the story?" Glorathy asked slightly threateningly, "You'll give me my own happy ending?" She didn't sound scornful now, just a bit mistrusting and hopeful.

I nodded. "I promise."

"You better keep that promise, girl," Glorathy said, "or you might have another inter-dimensional problem on your hands." The words sounded threatening, but there was an amused tone behind them, as if they were merely a joke. And maybe they were. With Glorathy, it was kind of hard to tell.

"So....what's the plan?" Jack asked, coming to stand next to me and use my shoulder as an elbow rest. Chloe and Dad approached too, a bit more hesitant, looking warily at Glorathy.

"I think I have an idea," I said.

Glorathy looked at me and raised an eyebrow in a manner that could only be described as impatient. "I'm listening..."

Six months later...

Brrrrrring! When the bell rang at the end of the day, on the first day back at school since the fictional invasion, in which the school was knocked down by a rampaging ogre, there was chaos. I waited at my desk for the flood of classmates to leave. The last to go were Katelyn and Josie, laughing about something. When they reached the door, Katelyn turned to look at me. I smiled and she smiled back. Then the two girls were gone, headed away to whatever they were doing next. And I didn't mind. For now, smiling was be enough.

"You ready to go?" came a familiar voice from beside me. I turned. Jack had already packed up his books and was standing beside his desk, waiting for me. He had quickly adjusted to being in a modern high school. Swiftly, I scraped together all of my stuff and shoved it into the appropriate places.

"Yeah, I'm ready," I told Jack, "Let's go."

Jack checked his smartphone, which was his new pride and joy, and said, "Mum's already here with Chloe."

Once we had arrived back in Christchurch with Jack, his mum, Malia, and his precious cow, the first thing Malia had wanted to do was learn to drive. Chloe had been teaching her for the past few months. Malia was on her way to getting her restricted license and she was very excited about it.

Jack and I wandered out into the hallway at a leisurely pace. It was nearly empty, as most students cleared out as soon as possible. As we strode down the hall, I spotted a girl who looked vaguely familiar. She had straight black hair and was reading a book while leaning against a row of lockers. It was the new girl I had seen on the day the portals started appearing. The girl who had smiled at me in the hall. When we passed, she glanced up. Meeting her gaze, I smiled and making a split second decision, headed over to the lockers. Jack followed me.

"Hi," I said, holding out a hand to shake hers. "I'm Cassie. This is Jack."

"Emmie," the girl said, lifting her hand to shake mine. As she did, I spotted the title of her book and had to smile.

...and the Beanstalk.

We talked for a while about nothing really. It was a little awkward, but it was okay.

"Hey, do you want to sit with us at lunch tomorrow?" I asked.

Emmie gave a wide grin. "Yeah, that'd be great. My mum will be so happy when I start making friends."

I smiled back. "Yeah, my mum will be too."

EPILOGUE

Warm summer sunlight filtered in through the windows of the quiet bookstore. The shop was empty, except for the crowded shelves, all loaded with books. A man stood attentively behind the counter, as if waiting for the next customer. After a few minutes passed, he relaxed a little and turned to the book he was reading, *The Hunger Games, Catching Fire.* He was interrupted from his reading by the cheerful ding of a bell as the shop door opened.

A young woman walked in, holding the hand of a little girl who yanked on her mother's arm, urging her towards the kids section. The woman exchanged a quick polite smile with the man behind the counter, then let her daughter lead her to the back of the bookstore. They searched for a while as the man watched them, but the girl did not pick out any books. As they headed towards the counter, the little girl complained loudly about not having found a book that she liked. As they passed the shelf at the front window, the mother stopped and picked up a book with a vibrant cover. The picture was of a girl with ocean blue hair and a little brown dog leaping through what appeared to be a swirling purple cloud, while an ominous gray haired woman loomed over them. The title flourished across the front cover. *The Trouble with Fiction.*

"I like that one, Mummy," the little girl said, reaching up to touch the book's shiny cover.

Her mother placed it on the counter. "We'll take this one."

The man glanced down at it and smiled. "We've had many requests for this book over the past month, but I've yet to read it. Maybe I should."

After the mother and her daughter had left, the man glanced at his half-finished *Hunger Games* book, then ducked around the counter to grab a copy of the book the woman had bought. He brought it back to the counter and opened it up to the first page.

Weak winter sunlight shone in through the windows of a quiet bookshop....

www.ingramcontent.com/pod-product-compliance
Lightning Source LLC
Chambersburg PA
CBHW070556120726
47909CB00007B/2357